Richard and Isab... ...t cultures. . .

Richard looked at Isab... ...h cheekbones, and her si... ...and he wanted to reach out and kiss her. He pushed back her hair and cupped the back of her neck. He gave it the slightest pressure, feeling her body shiver from his touch. "Oh, Isabella, I—"

"Don't, don't say it, Richard. We can't."

Richard shook his head. "I'm sorry." How stupid could he be? Her father would be furious. He'd given his word he wouldn't act in an improper way toward Isabella, and here he was about to kiss her senseless. But she wanted him to. Regret gathered in her eyes.

"I'm sorry, Isabella. It won't happen again."

"But. . ."

"No, Isabella, I need you to work for me. I can't ruin that by allowing my emotions to take control. If I kissed you, your father would never permit you to come and work for me again."

"Unless you married me."

LYNN A. COLEMAN is a Martha's Vineyard native who now calls the tropics of Miami, Florida, home. She is a minister's wife who writes to the Lord's glory through the various means of articles, short stories, and a web site. She has three grown children and six grandchildren.

She also hosts an inspirational romance writing workshop on the Internet, manages an inspirational romance web site, edits an inspirational romance electronic newsletter, and serves as president of the American Christian Romance Writers organization.

HEARTSONG PRESENTS

One Man's Honor

Lynn A. Coleman

Heartsong Presents

To Jonathan and Joshua, my twin grandsons, who were the original inspiration behind Richie in A Time to Embrace. *May you two grow up to be strong and honorable men for God. This is my prayer.*

Love,
Grandma

A note from the author:
I love to hear from my readers! You may correspond with me by writing:
Lynn A. Coleman
Author Relations
PO Box 719
Uhrichsville, OH 44683

ISBN 1-58660-487-2

ONE MAN'S HONOR

Cover illustration by Dick Bobnick.

PRINTED IN THE U.S.A.

one

Key West, April 1, 1886

"Fire! Fire!"

Richard Southard jumped from his bed and ran down the stairs, rushing to answer the pounding fist on his front door.

"Your dock's on fire!" The young man's eyes bulged. "And your warehouse." He gasped for breath.

Richard sniffed the air. "Thanks." His dock was on fire? *Lord, have mercy.* "I'll get some buckets," he mumbled.

"Don't think they'll do much good. Half the town's on fire." The man turned and leapt off the porch.

"Would you go tell Mo Greene for me?" Richard didn't wait for an answer and rushed up the stairs two at a time.

"What's all the hootin' and hollerin' for?" Cook grumbled, tightening the old bathrobe around her.

"Town's on fire, Cook. You better stay here. Get some buckets of water ready to dampen some rags for breathing through."

"Lord protect us," Cook groaned. She'd been with the family since before he arrived on Key West, as the housekeeper and cook for his uncle. But, in point of fact, she'd been the closest person he ever had to a grandparent.

"Amen." Richard finished his hike up the stairs, removing his robe before entering his room. No time to undress and dress. He slipped his clothes on over his nightshirt, shoved his feet into his boots, then ran toward the family dock and business. His uncle Ellis had developed a healthy sponge fishing industry on Key West. Richard had returned to Key West last fall to work the family business while Ellis and his family returned to New York.

Thick smoke drove Richard from his thoughts. The

warehouse glowed in the early morning hour. The wind continued to whip the flames up as they licked the leaves of palm trees. Drying sponges became soft cannonballs of flame.

The single fire truck could never handle this.

Richard coughed. The acrid taste of smoke burned his throat and eyes. He tore off the bottom of his nightshirt and fashioned a mask to breathe through.

He scanned the long dock that worked its way into the harbor. Fire on the ocean—what an incredible sight! Dry season was not the time for the island to have a fire. They hadn't had rain on Key West for weeks, perhaps months.

Richard pulled off his outer shirt and soaked it with ocean water. At least he could try and stop the balls of fire that were being spread by the sponges blowing off his roof. He ran after a sponge fireball and slapped it several times with his drenched shirt.

"What happened?" Mo Greene called out.

Richard jumped hearing Mo's voice. He turned to see the tall black man's stride slow down. "I don't know. I found the place like this. But look up Duval Street; everything is on fire. There are five docks on fire counting ours," Richard informed him.

"Ain't seen nothin' like this in all my days."

"Won't have many days if you don't put something over your nose and mouth." Mo stood head and shoulders above most men. He had worked for Richard's uncle since Richard was a small boy. Mo and Lizzy's children had been his playmates. Now Richard was Mo's boss. Somehow it seemed odd, telling Mo what to do, especially when Mo had had a hand in correcting him a time or two when he was a young boy growing up on the island.

Mo removed a handkerchief and wet it with ocean water, draping it over his nose and mouth. "Want me to try and save the dock?" he yelled. The roar of the wind and flames made his normal voice a hoarse whisper.

Richard shook his head no. "We need to stop the sponges from starting more fires. The dock should burn itself out."

Mo removed his shirt. Dampening it, he filled a couple buckets he'd brought along with him. They each took a bucket and proceeded to chase the sponge fireballs.

Hours later, they sat exhausted, breathing in fresher air as the sun crested the horizon. The winds had shifted. The stale smell of burned wood hung in the air, but it was more breathable.

Hundreds of men had come out to battle the flames, but their efforts did little good. Ironically, the town had decided not to upgrade the fire department the previous year. Richard knew that would change immediately. "Day late and a dollar short," he mumbled.

"Huh?" Mo asked.

"Sorry, was thinking about the single fire engine. The town will need another. Our population is nearly as large as Jacksonville. One fire engine isn't enough."

"I helped your uncle build this building. Hard to believe it could be destroyed so easily."

"Buildings can be rebuilt. It's the people I'm worried about. I pray no lives were lost tonight."

"Amen. I'm going home to freshen up. I'll be back in a few hours to help clean up."

"Thanks, Mo."

Mo lifted his massive dark frame and slowly walked away. Richard could not help but be amazed all over again at the man's depth, how hard he'd worked to educate himself and improve his speech.

Richard turned and looked at the smoldering remains of the family business. Should they rebuild? The last letter from Nanna and Ellis said they were reconsidering staying in New York and using the house on Key West as a winter home.

There was no question his uncle was beginning to slow down. That would leave Richard and his cousin James in charge of the family business. Richard gnawed his lower lip.

The question was whether he wanted to run this business, go west and explore the new territories, or return to the farmstead? He'd been working the land for five years. He enjoyed it. He had a natural talent for farming, like his father before him. So what was he doing in Key West? Why had it seemed so important to stay here and keep the sponge business going? His uncle had plenty of offers to buy the business. Richard looked at the rubble and sighed.

"Richard." Micah Bower worked his lean body through the charred remains. "You've been hit hard."

"How'd your place fare?"

"We're fine. The fire didn't get that far east. Glad we purchased the new location five years ago." Micah sat down beside him, his clothes streaked with smoke. Richard gazed down at his own clothing. The soot and smoke had stained his nightshirt.

"Have you been up Duval Street?"

"Nope. How bad is it?"

"Looks like fifty buildings and five docks went up. The fire spread down to Greene Street."

"Fifty?" Richard sighed. "How'd it start?"

"No one knows, but they're looking into it."

"Are you going to rebuild?" Micah scanned the debris.

"Yes, James is planning on returning to Key West after his education. I'll need to reestablish the business so he has something to come home to."

Micah nodded. "It's going to take some time to rebuild. I can't imagine how long."

"Or how many shipments of supplies. Thankfully, there are a few docks still standing."

"There are some drawbacks to living on an island."

"Why did you stay on Key West?" Richard knew Micah was around his own age when he'd come to the island.

"At first I wanted, and needed, time to get to know my mother, to reconcile what had transpired in our lives. But after a few years I found the island and its people growing on me. Although I must say, there are far more folks living here now, almost too many."

Richard smiled and acknowledged he had similar thoughts.

"After I met Catherine there was no question. I was staying for awhile longer," Micah grinned.

"Ah, a woman will do that to ya."

"And what do you know of women?" Micah challenged.

Richard raised his hands. "Not a thing. Trust me, I've kept myself away from them. I have too many demands on my time; I don't need a woman messing up my life."

Micah roared. "That, my friend, is simply because you haven't met the right one yet."

Richard examined the soot on his friend. "You might want to jump in the ocean before you return home to Catherine and the children. They'll never recognize you."

"Cook might have trouble recognizing you when you get home too."

"Oh no, I forgot about Cook." Richard jumped up. "She's eighty now, not that you'd know it by looking at her. This air had to be difficult on her breathing."

"Take care, Richard. I'll lend a hand when I can."

Richard watched Micah wave as he rounded the corner and headed down Front Street. Thankfully, his house was east of the fire. Richard coughed as his lungs fought to recover from the smoke he'd inhaled. "Lord, please let her be okay."

"Cook!" he hollered as he ran through the front door.

No response. "Cook!" he yelled louder. Frantic, he ran to the back bedroom. He paused and tried to calm himself before opening the door. *If she died. . .*

He steeled himself and pushed it open. A sigh of relief passed his lips as he saw her empty bed and room.

"Richie," Cook called.

Her voice carried from the backyard. Richard ran down the hall, skidding on the throw rug on the well-polished oak floor. How many times had his uncle and nanna scolded him about running in the hallway? A wicked grin creased his face. *Too many,* he answered himself.

"Cook, are you all right?"

He saw her bent over, carrying a bucket of water from the cistern. Her natural brown color seemed paler this morning—or could it be a contrast to the black charred remains of the fire? "Let me get that for you."

"You're a mess. Take them clothes off, what's left of 'em, and get yourself cleaned up," she ordered.

Richard chuckled and scooped up her bucket. "Yes, Ma'am."

"Have ya seen yourself?" She applied a loving hand on his elbow. He could feel the unsteady gait as she walked beside him. She claimed bones just had a way of stiffening up, getting ready to lie down for eternity.

"No, but I've seen others. Couldn't imagine how Mo could look darker than he is naturally. But he sure was black."

Cook chuckled. "He's a dark one, all right. You're just about his equal with all that soot on ya."

"Closest I'll ever get, I imagine." Richard's pale complexion never really tanned. He did have a tan, though most wouldn't know it. Blond hair, blue eyes, and pale skin weren't exactly tropical colors for a body.

"Well ya stink, too, so go wash up."

"Yes, Ma'am." The woman could scold him from sun up to sun down if she wanted. She was safe, and that's all that mattered.

He put the bucket in the kitchen and went behind the house to the outside shower. *No sense getting this soot in a tub. I'd only have to clean it out later,* he reasoned.

Cook lifted the window above him. "Catch."

She tossed him a clean washrag and a bar of soap.

"Thanks."

"How bad was the fire?" she asked. He could hear her dragging a chair to the window.

"Bad, real bad." He lathered his skin, amazed at the gray mounds of soap bubbles coming off him. "Micah Bower says pretty near fifty buildings went up and five docks. We lost the dock and the building. Everything will have to be rebuilt."

"God protect us! How many folks you suppose'll be outta work?"

"Quite a few, but I imagine they'll be hired to help rebuild. I know I'll have our men doing that." He poured some water over his head and lathered his hair with the soap.

"Anyone hurt?"

"Don't know. I can't imagine folks not getting injured with that much destruction. I had to wear a mask most of the time I was down there. The air was so thick."

"Mercy." In his mind's eye, he could see the old woman folding her hands and offering another prayer.

Cook was not a person to try and pull the wool over someone's eyes, but she was also one of the strongest prayer warriors going. Maybe he should tell her his dilemma. He could use the extra prayer support. He opened his mouth, then clamped it shut. Nope, he was a man now, and a man needed to make certain decisions on his own.

"What are you going to do, Richie?"

"First I'll need to clean up the mess. Then I'll need to rebuild. The business needs to be in order for James's return."

"I'm sure Mo will be happy to hear you're going to rebuild."

Mo—he'd almost forgotten. Six men and their families depended on his family business. *Lord, I feel so ill equipped. I know I've had the book learning about running a business, but that's not enough. Uncle Ellis always said that if you were good to your employees, they would work well for you. You couldn't just give them everything; they'd have to earn it. But being generous, whenever possible, would produce loyal workers. I can't dispute that, Lord. Mo's been working for the company for nearly twenty years. Help me, Lord. I don't know where to begin.*

"Richie?"

"Yes, Cook." Richard rinsed his body off one last time.

"Ifin ya don't mind, I'm goin' to lie down. I've been up since you left."

"No problem. I'll be in town most of the day myself. Don't bother to cook for me. I'll find something."

"There're a couple loaves of Cuban bread in the bread box. You might want to take one and some cheese. Drink plenty of water too. Cleaning up from a fire isn't easy work."

"Yes, Ma'am." Richard wrapped a towel around his waist and dumped his clothes into a barrel, then filled it with some water and lye soap. Cook would have his hide because he washed his own clothes, but she didn't need the extra work. Besides, he knew the fresh clothing he'd put on later would be just as filthy, if not more so, after working at the shop.

❧

Digging through the debris certainly proved he would be black again. He salvaged a few knives, sponge hooks, and various pieces from the shop, but basically the entire business was lost. The schooner, the *Sea Dove*, and half a dozen of the spongers' skiffs, were safe, along with the tools from the boat.

A trip to Cuba might be in order. He'd certainly get the building supplies he needed sooner. Richard sat down on the edge of the seawall in front of the burned-out building. Reaching into his sack, he pulled out the Cuban bread.

"I'm a fish out of water, Lord." Richard tossed a piece of his Cuban roll into the water, then bit off a piece for himself. The soft white bread with a thin crust had been a food item he'd missed. "Who am I, Lord? The farmer or a businessman?"

Richard tossed another chunk of the bread into the water and watched a small school of fish fight for the tasty morsel. The brightly colored parrotfish jumped out of the water, chasing the elusive crumb. Although Key West was in turmoil after the fire, the fish under the sea seemed free from such hardships. He'd heard four people had died.

The gentle lull of a feminine voice teased his ears. "Cast thy bread upon the waters: for thou shalt find it after many days."

Richard turned and caught a glimpse of her as she headed away from him into town, a lily among the ruins. Her wavy black hair draped over a clean, crisp, white blouse. Her golden skin was vibrant among the mounds of charred debris. The familiar passage from Ecclesiastes echoed in his mind. He looked down at the loaf of bread, pulled off another chunk, and tossed it in the waters below.

"Could it be that simple, Lord?"

two

Isabella turned, sneaking another glimpse of Richie Southard, or at least she thought it was him. He'd returned to Key West after being gone for five years. She'd been on the island for six. She had been all of fourteen when she first spotted him working with his uncle at the dock. He was handsome then, but now. . .well, she wouldn't allow her thoughts to drift in that direction.

He seemed so alone. She knew she shouldn't have spoken to him. It wasn't proper, but. . . *I just couldn't help myself.*

She scanned the ruins from the great fire. The town was decimated. Her father's cigar factory was gone. In fact, several cigar factories were gone.

She needed to get a job. She'd been trying for what seemed like eternity but hadn't found work to her liking. Oh, she'd cleaned houses and done other simple tasks, but a desire stirred deep within her to do something more, to be something more. But what?

Now the town would be set on rebuilding, and construction wasn't something she felt skilled at or inclined to do. Not that any man would hire her even if she applied. With her head for numbers, she'd hoped to get a job at a bank. With her bilingual abilities, she figured she would be welcomed. Instead, she found no job openings anywhere. Not even a sales clerk opportunity had presented itself. Every day she'd come to town, and every day she'd returned home without a job.

Should she be trusting God with the same passage of Scripture she'd tossed out to Richie Southard?

Isabella took in a deep breath and practically gagged from

the ash-laden air. Small patches of debris still had fine trails of smoke floating upward. "Lord, what am I going to do? There'll be no work for my father, and I haven't found a job. What's the family going to do?"

A thought flickered through her mind that she should trust the Lord and leave the concerns of the family in His care, not hers. But she fought off the idea. She had to do something, anything. Her family depended upon her. Her father had not been blessed with a son, and she was the only child. She had little to offer, other than marrying well. . . . Richie Southard's blue-gray eyes, crowned with a riot of golden curls, passed in front of her mind's eye. *No, I couldn't do that,* she reprimanded herself.

She couldn't even get a job at the cigar factory where her father worked. He had been most adamant that his daughter not work with the tobacco. He did it because it paid the bills. "No, you shall marry a good husband, and God will provide for you," he'd always say. Which is why, at age twenty and still not married, she desperately needed employment. If she didn't find a job soon, Papá would find her a husband.

"Isabella."

She turned to find Mariella carrying her young son Miguel and pulling her daughter Rosetta along with her. "Isn't this such a horrible disaster?"

"Sí." Mariella still spoke Spanish, but she primarily used English now. "What are you doing down here with the children?"

"My curiosity got the best of me. I couldn't stand it waiting at home." Mariella pushed her long dark hair behind her shoulders.

Isabella smiled. "Me too. Have you heard how it started?"

"No, just rumors. Some say it was Cuban businessmen who wanted to stop the production of the cigars here."

"But didn't they move up to Tampa?"

"Sí, but they also don't like competition. Who knows if it

was them or some of the other wild rumors floating around. Everything is so dry here. The buildings were all wood, with wooden roofs. . . . It just spread so fast."

"It's amazing no one was injured."

Mariella reached out and placed her hand on her forearm. "You haven't heard? Four men lost their lives."

"Oh, no. Who?"

"I don't know. I guess they're waiting to have a positive identification before they say anything to anyone."

"Dear Jesus, be with their families," Isabella prayed out loud.

"Amen." Mariella adjusted Miguel on her hip.

"How's your aunt Peg's business? Did it get burned?" Peg Bower owned a small shop of various items crafted by islanders. Her own specialty was beautiful embroidery work.

"Her store is fine. Uncle Matt's dock and buildings are fine too. Micah came by early this morning and let us know. Miguel is happy he still has a job."

"I can imagine. The Southard's dock and building are destroyed."

"I wonder how Richie is going to handle this. He's come back with all that college learning, and I haven't seen a change in the business. Don't get me wrong, Ellis Southard built up a fine business, but to put it in Richie's hands and just leave the island like that. . . . The man must have been crazy. But Mo Greene still works for him, so that's a blessing."

Isabella had heard the gossip before about folks not expecting much from Richie and his fancy college education. She'd often thought people's concerns were more about his age rather than his abilities. "Seems to me he managed his farmstead just fine for five years."

"I don't know. Why did Ellis have to go to New York if it hadn't been for some mismanagement on Richie's part? After all, he let Richie go there by himself for his education. Why not let James do the same?"

This was the foundation for the gossip. "I'd prefer to give

Richie the benefit of the doubt. Besides, what are the other businessmen going to do now that their businesses have been destroyed?"

"You know, you're probably right. After all, Richie's been running the business for eight months now and kept everyone gainfully employed, plus hired a couple more hands."

See, Isabella wanted to boast but bit her tongue. It had to be difficult on Richard to have the whole town thinking he was inept at running the business, even though he'd proved himself over the past eight months. This fire would definitely be another test for him to endure. She shot another prayer heavenward for Richard Southard. *Give him strength, Lord.* She picked up a charred board.

"Put that down," Mariella scolded. "I better get these *niños* home before they are as black as some of the men working in the rubble. Good to see you, Isabella. Come over for tea sometime."

❧

"Mo, I'm going to take the *Sea Dove* to Cuba and load her up with supplies." Richard glanced over at the white-hulled two-masted schooner glistening in the harbor. He turned his gaze back on the remains of the warehouse. "Will you take care of the cleanup?"

"Whatever you need, Richard."

"Thanks. I'll take a couple of men with me to help sail and load the vessel. I'm not sure how much she can handle, but we'll load her as full as we can."

"You be careful. Two trips are better than one if you and the ship end up lying on the bottom," Mo warned.

"Don't worry. I'm impulsive but not stupid."

"Never said you were, Son. Just don't push it. I know you're under a lot of pressure to prove yourself, and this here fire ain't gonna help none. Just remember, God doesn't give us more than we can handle."

Richard reached up and grabbed Mo's shoulder. "Thanks,

Mo. I appreciate that. Will you keep an eye out for your mother-in-law for me? I'm sure you would anyway, but she's getting on now."

"Of course. Lizzy and I will take care of her. Tried to get her to move in with us, but she wouldn't hear of it. And with my mother having a small room to herself, I'm sure Francine would feel she was imposing. She wouldn't be, but she'd feel that way. Heard even George asked her to move in with them." Mo grinned. "But she insists she needs to take care of you."

"She's always been there as long as I can remember. The house would definitely not be the same if she were to move out. I could manage just fine on my own, but you won't catch me telling her that."

Mo laughed. "What would be the point?"

"Exactly," Richard chuckled.

"You've been doing a fine job, Richard. Don't let what the island gossips say get ya none." Mo placed his hand on Richard's shoulder this time.

"Thanks, I try not to listen to them but. . ."

"They're like the constant buzz of a mosquito you can't swat fast enough." Mo chuckled and swatted an invisible bug swarming around his head.

"Yeah."

"I know. Lizzy and I had to deal with them a time or two. Not much a man can do other than to do his best before God. Everyone else really doesn't matter."

"I'll keep that in mind. Now, I better get a move on so I can set sail with the tide."

Richard hadn't been too surprised to see no one show up this morning to work. Yet there really wasn't any reason why they couldn't go sponging. But where would he dry the sponges if they had collected them? He worked his way through town and found some of his men helping to remove the debris. He gave them orders to report to Mo or himself in the morning. At home, he washed and packed for his ocean voyage. Back in the office, he sat at his uncle's desk and worked out the materials he would need to rebuild the warehouse and dock.

A gentle knock on the door broke his thoughts. "Come in, Cook."

"I brought ya some hot coffee, Richie."

"Thanks. Have a seat."

Cook slowly settled her aging body in the chair opposite him. She'd always been so active; it hurt to see her less than agile.

"Don't you go frettin' 'bout my old bones, Boy. I may take a little more time doin' this or that, but I'm still getting around on my own steam, which is more than I can say 'bout some my age."

"Cook, you'll never change. How'd you know I was thinking that?"

"I've known you since you were less than three feet high. I suspect I know ya pretty well."

"I suspect you're right." Richard leaned back in the office chair behind his desk.

"Whatcha workin' on?"

"The figures for the materials needed to rebuild the warehouse. I'm going to order brick and mortar. If there's a fire again, I don't want the whole building going up."

"Wise decision."

"I'm tempted to put in more windows for better ventilation, but that gives more room for someone to break in. Not that stealing a ton of sponges wouldn't be hard to get away with."

"What would your uncle Ellis do?"

"I don't know."

"Well then, I guess it's up to you. He trusts ya, Richie. He knows you'll make the right decision."

Richard tapped his pen on the papers he'd been working on. "It's just that—" A knock at the front door broke his ramblings.

"Wonder who that is?"

"Stay right there, Cook. I'll get it." Richard hurried to the front door. "Yes, may I help you?"

A group of five men stood on his front porch. Some were men he recognized; others he didn't.

"Mr. Southard, we heard you were going to Havana to purchase some building materials. We'd like to secure passage on your schooner. We need to do the same."

"Come in, Gentlemen. The schooner has been stripped of any cabins. It's strictly a boat for hauling."

"We don't care," a thin man with a razor-straight nose said as they walked past him into the hallway.

"The thing is, Mr. Southard, we all need supplies," Ben Greely piped in.

"True. Take a seat in the parlor, Gentlemen. Let's see what we can work out. Make yourselves comfortable. I'll be right in."

The men streamed into the front room, and Richard went back to his office. "Who was it?" Cook asked.

"Some men from town wanting to book passage on the *Sea Dove*. Can you make us some coffee, Cook?"

"Certainly."

"Thanks." Richard took some fresh pieces of paper, plus some pens and ink out to the front parlor. "All right, Gentlemen, let's see what we can do."

All six looked at him with amazement. One older man with white hair and a balding top rolled his eyes. Obviously, paper and pens reminded him of Richard's fancy college education.

"Here's the situation. My ship is small. I can handle a very limited amount of weight. However, the suppliers in Havana have their own shipping vessels. I can take your purchase orders just as easily."

David Zachary leaned forward and took a sheet of paper. "Sounds good to me."

Another knock jarred the front door. "Excuse me, Gentlemen."

"I heard you were going to Havana?" a Hispanic gentleman asked.

"Yes."

"May I come? I have family in Cuba I haven't seen in a long time. I would be deeply in your debt if you would let me travel with you."

"Come in. I'm working on the details of the trip with others. Take a seat in the front parlor."

Richard noticed a stream of people making its way toward his house or front door. "Just come on in," he hollered and joined the men in the parlor.

"Looks like you folks aren't the only ones. If you trust me, I'll bring your orders to the suppliers. But I only have limited room for passengers."

Each man took a sheet of paper and began to write their list.

"Before you write your lists, let me tell you my plans. I'm going to rebuild the warehouse with brick. This will help protect against a future fire."

"Hmm, you might be on to something there." Ben tapped the end of the pen against his chin. "I think I'll do the same."

The rest of the evening was filled with other guests making similar requests. Most gave their orders to Richard; a few wanted to travel to see family. But when they found out he was only staying for one day in Cuba, they decided not to go at this time. By the time he went to bed, he had twenty orders and two extra passengers.

He penned a letter to his uncle and explained about the fire and his plans to rebuild.

Later, as his mind drifted off to sleep, the memory of the lily of the ruins brought a smile to his face.

❧

"You're going to Cuba?" Isabella couldn't believe her ears.

"Sí, I must visit your grandmother."

"But, Papá, what about work? The fire?"

"It does not matter. There is no work right now, and I can visit your grandmother."

"But, Papá, what about rebuilding the factory? There will be work, sí?"

"Sí, but Mr. Southard is ordering the supplies for the men. If I go with him, I will return with the supplies. Then I can work when I return."

That made sense. "May I go, Papá? I would love to see Grandmother."

"I don't know, *Niña.* A boat with a bunch of sailors is not the place for a beautiful woman such as yourself."

"Oh, Papá, I don't care about the sailors. I only wish to see Grandmother."

Her father looked over to her mother. His silver-streaked sideburns made him more handsome in his later years. Isabella fought down a grin; she knew she was getting to him. Whenever he looked to her mother, Isabella knew she'd convinced her father. Her mother wasn't as easy to sway. "Oh please, Mima. It's been so long since we've seen Grandmother."

"I don't know, Isabella. Your father makes a point about the sailors."

"But, Mima, are they really sailors or just some of Mr. Southard's employees? I mean, it is his boat."

The idea of traveling with Richard Southard to Cuba excited and frightened Isabella all at the same time. Would he say anything about her speaking to him earlier today?

Her mother put down her sewing. Her dark brown eyes examined Isabella's. "How do you know Mr. Southard?"

"I pass his warehouse every day I go into town. It's not hard to miss a man with yellow ringlets of hair." *And the most incredible blue-gray eyes I've ever seen,* she added silently.

"You have spoken with Mr. Southard?"

Ah, the real issue. Should she lie? Should she tell the truth and face certain punishment? "Not really, Mima."

"And what is that supposed to mean?" She saw her father stiffen.

"I merely quoted a verse of Scripture as I passed by this morning. He was tossing pieces of bread into the water and I quoted Ecclesiastes to him. He seemed so tired. The fire destroyed everything of his business. Even his dock."

"I see. And you've not addressed him other than this?"

"No, Mima."

"Yolanda, what is the harm in quoting Scripture to a man?" her father asked.

"Nothing." Her mother's eyes narrowed. *She knows*, Isabella thought.

"May I go, Mima?"

"Sí, but you must not speak with Mr. Southard if you are alone. Only when your father is around."

"Sí, Mima, I promise."

three

Richard tossed his satchel in the captain's quarters and stepped out onto the deck. He'd packed all his cash from the safe to order his supplies; hopefully, it would be enough. The galley was loaded with fresh water and provisions for the small crew. Emile Fernandez approached him with a barrel of what Richard assumed was fresh water.

"Buenos días, Señor Southard, como está?"

"Bien, and you?"

"Bien, thank you for asking."

"I wish to ask an additional favor from you. My daughter would like to travel with us to visit her grandmother. If you see it in your heart to let her go, I shall pay for her."

"Mr. Fernandez, the *Sea Dove* is not a place for *niñas.*"

"Isabella is a young woman."

Richard could not allow a woman to travel on such a ship as this. He opened his mouth to protest.

"My daughter, she knows this is not a pleasure cruise. She understands. I shall be with her whenever she is on deck. I know I am asking a tremendous favor, but her grandmother, she is old and we don't know—"

"All right, all right." Richard raised his hands in surrender. "But tell her I want no complaints about her lack of comfort."

"Sí, muchas gracias, Señor."

"De nada."

Just what he needed, a spoiled young lady on board. Richard went forward to check the rigging.

"Richard, the food's stored below. You should have plenty, even with your extra guests." Mo smirked.

"You heard?"

24

"Yessa, and I'm sure glad I'm not the captain of this here trip." Mo looped his thumbs around the waistband of his trousers.

"You know, Mo, I don't see any reason why you couldn't take the trip. I could manage the men on shore."

"Sorry, Richard, my wife would have my hide ifin I didn't return for several days. Come now, I know you'll find Isabella's a fine young lady."

"Fine spoiled young lady."

"Perhaps." Mo smirked again and quickly went over the edge, slipping down into the skiff below.

"Chicken."

Mo simply roared with laughter.

Who is this Isabella Fernandez, anyway? He'd never spoken with Emile before last night, and there were so many people on Key West now that he couldn't possibly know everyone.

Richard climbed the mast to the yardarm and examined the rigging. A hooded creature in a skirt scurried on board and went down below. *Perhaps a woman to cook the meals wouldn't be such a bad thing after all,* he mused.

He climbed down the rigging and, having thoroughly examined the boat, he ordered, "Raise the mainsail." The massive sail fluttered in the wind. "Hoist the anchor."

Richard grabbed the wheel and nudged it until the wind caught the sail. He navigated the ship out of the harbor as if he were walking down the street. He knew the waters and the reefs around the small island like the trees in the garden behind his house. Once out of the harbor, he looked at his compass and set a course for Havana. Ninety miles due south or there about. Richard enjoyed the rush of wind to welcome him back to the open sea. Sailing would definitely be one of the things he'd miss if he moved back to New York.

"Take the helm, Ben. I'm going to my cabin to work on the various orders." Ben Greely had been one of the two who decided to join him on his trip.

"With pleasure, Captain." A grin quirked Richard's lips as he headed toward the captain's quarters. He wasn't sure how necessary it really was for Ben to travel to Cuba, but the man seemed to genuinely love the sea.

Before entering his cabin, he paused. *Should I check on our other guests? Nope, this isn't a pleasure cruise, and I'm not their host.* He opened the door to his small quarters and pulled out the attaché with each man's orders. Some of the men had given him contacts in Cuba, folks with whom they'd done business before. Others had given him deposits for their orders, while still others had promised their word was as good as gold. Richard checked and rechecked the figures, making a master list of items needed and a secondary list of who had ordered what.

Hours later, he worked the crick out of his neck, massaging it. The gentle whiff of something cooking made his stomach gurgle. Yes, allowing a woman on board wasn't a bad decision, he mused.

He dropped his pen into its holder and gathered his papers, putting them back into the waterproof attaché. He couldn't afford to have these papers destroyed by water. He placed the attaché in the secret safe with his money and followed his nose to the galley.

"Smelling mighty fine, isn't it, Captain?" Ben smiled.

"Sure is. Who ever said a woman wasn't welcome on a ship ought to have their heads examined."

Ben chuckled. "Miss Isabella ain't too bad on the eyes, either."

"What?"

"You haven't met her?" Ben raised his eyebrows and strained to keep a smile from his face.

"No. Emile asked this morning. I was up on the yardarm when she came on board."

"You're in for a treat, my friend."

Just great. He didn't need a beautiful woman on board stirring his men's thoughts in the wrong direction. Then again, most of his crew were family men. He had to keep reminding himself he wasn't on a ship with a bunch of earthy seamen. These were just his employees and a couple businessmen from Key West. Besides, with Emile on board, a man would be foolish to bring on a father's wrath. If the hood over her head was any indication, Miss Isabella had been raised in a very strict and old-fashioned Spanish home.

"Personally, I don't care what she looks like. I'm more interested in that heavenly aroma coming from the galley. I've never smelled anything so fine coming from down there."

Ben chuckled. "Never brought Cook along?"

"Nope. She always said if the good Lord wanted us on the water, He'd have given us fins. Of course, she likes to sail every once in awhile. She just isn't partial to long sea voyages."

"Ah, well, no one could ever make Cook do anything she didn't want to," Ben quipped.

"You're telling me? I grew up under that woman's hand. Trust me, I know."

Ben chuckled again. "Keep forgetting that she lives in your place."

"Shall I bring you something up or would you like me to relieve you for a spell?" Richard asked.

"I'm fine, had a big breakfast. After you've eaten, I'll go down."

"Okay, I'll be back shortly."

"Don't rush on my account. I love sailing." With a feather touch, Ben guided the helm.

"I can tell. You know, I might be in need of a captain for a spell to ship my orders. You interested?"

"I'll think on it. Generally, my business keeps me in port."

Richard nodded and headed toward the galley.

"What smells so good. . . ?" His voice trailed off. The lily of the ruins was aboard the *Sea Dove*.

Lord, help me.

ʚ

"Mr. Southard, this is my daughter, Isabella."

Isabella watched Richard slowly close his lips, turn inquiringly to her father, then back to her.

"Buenos días, Isabella, como está?"

"Bien, muchas gracías for letting me travel with you. I promise to stay out of the way. Father suggested I help out by making the meals. Is that a problem?"

"No, no, not at all, unless you consider the fact that the good smells will have my crew's stomachs rumbling for hours before they can eat." Richard smiled. His blue-gray eyes darkened a touch. "And what did you make that smells so good?"

"Asopado de mariscos."

"Smells great. May I have some?"

Isabella fumbled for a bowl and scooped out a healthy portion of the fish and rice stew. *Lord, help me not pay him too much attention.*

"When do you expect to arrive in Havana?" her father asked Richard as he sat down at the small table.

The men's hammocks hung behind the galley. She'd examined the ship, discovering there wasn't a private room for herself and her father. She would have to hang a canvas or blanket to create some privacy.

"If the winds hold, I'm hoping to arrive late tonight. Mr. Fernandez—"

"Emile," her father corrected.

"Emile, I'm afraid we're going to have to change the sleeping arrangements. There isn't a private room on ship, except for the captain's quarters, and I insist that Isabella stay in there. I'll bunk below with the men."

"No, Señor Southard, we cannot impose."

Oh Father, why do you insist on. . . No, he was right. They were not passengers; they were simply glorified stowaways.

"No, Señor Fernandez, I insist. I can't put your daughter in such a compromising situation. You may not be aware, but there is no privacy for her. I thought perhaps you and your daughter could stay in the bow, and I'd have the men move the sails, but I think my quarters are the better choice and easier all the way around."

Isabella handed him the bowl of *asopado de mariscos*.

"Muchas gracías."

Isabella nodded and sat down beside her father. "I wouldn't want to impose."

"No imposition. I will have to use the desk a time or two before we arrive, but I'll try and do that while you're on deck or cooking down below. That is, if you wish to continue cooking. This is wonderful."

"Thank you." She folded her hands in her lap, hiding her sweaty palms. Why did this golden-haired man affect her so?

"You're very kind, Mr. Southard. . . ."

"Richard," he corrected her father with a smile.

Lord, You made him with such a wonderful smile. Isabella blinked away her wayward thoughts as her fingers fumbled along the edge of her apron.

A grin raised the furrowed lines of her father's face. "Richard, have you figured out how much material you're ordering?"

"Some. I need to finalize the figures. Are you familiar with some good men to do business with in Havana?"

"I'd be honored to help you. I shall ask around. And my cousin Manuel—he sells building supplies."

"Thank you. The men gave me several contacts with whom they've done business before."

"Sí, that is good."

Richard lifted his bowl to spoon out the remaining stew. "Exquisite *asopado de mariscos*, thank you." He sliced off a hunk of bread and cheese. "I'll have my quarters ready in an hour."

"Muchas gracías, Mr. Southard."

She watched him climb the ladder.

"He's a good man," her father whispered.

"Sí."

Isabella cleaned up Richard's dishes and fed the other men as they came down. Staying in the captain's quarters would make this trip much more pleasurable, and the view from the stern windows would be wonderful.

"Isabella?"

"Sí, Padre?"

"I'm going to carry your baggage up to the captain's quarters. Do you wish to come up on deck with me?"

"Sí." She couldn't wait to breathe in the fresh air. The galley wasn't bad, but the heat from the small stove and poor ventilation from the small window didn't provide much comfort.

The bright sun danced on the deep blue ocean. They were several hours south of Key West now. The sun arced high in the sky, and the brush of the wind on her face caused her to stretch her arms out to cool down her body.

"Isabella," her father spoke sharply under his breath.

"I'm sorry, Papá, I wasn't thinking." A woman did not flaunt herself in such a way. She followed behind him as he made his way to the captain's quarters. It was a small room set in the stern. Her father knocked before entering.

The room was empty; the bed, freshly made. A small brown leather pouch sat on the desk, *which also serves as a table,* she surmised.

"Where would you like these?" her father asked.

"Put them on the bed, Papá. I'll unpack a dress for tomorrow and leave the rest for our visit with Grandmother."

"Sí, that is wise. Do you wish for me to sleep in here?"

Isabella looked around the small cabin. He'd have to sleep on the floor, unless there was a hammock she didn't know about. "No, Papá, I'll be safe. There's a lock on the door."

"I'll stay with you until it's time to retire this evening."

"I would like your company. Maybe Mr. Southard has a chess board or something for us to pass the time."

"I shall ask him while you unpack."

Isabella went right to work. She removed a long cotton skirt and a white cotton blouse for tomorrow. She hung them in the small closet, where she found what she presumed were Richard's clothes. A quick glance over her shoulder told her she was alone, and then she reached for his dark blue suit coat and smelled it. *Oh, Lord, help me. I'm attracted to this man in a way that would not be pleasing to my parents or to our customs.* She dropped the coat sleeve as if it singed her fingers. For her own personal sanity, she would have to find ways to limit her contact with one Richard Southard. *But how can I do that on a ship?*

❧

Richard stood at the helm and sailed the ship into Havana Harbor. The trip had been uneventful. Having arrived late in the evening, he'd anchored just outside the harbor. Isabella's fine cooking made the journey all the more pleasurable. He'd thanked the Lord on more than one occasion that she'd stayed out of the way. Last evening he'd almost gone to her when he saw her standing on the bow, but something stopped him. He prayed it was good common sense. Emile Fernandez guarded his daughter like a hawk. A man would be foolish to attempt a one-on-one meeting with her. Growing up in Key West had allowed him to learn of some of the strong Hispanic customs some of the families practiced. Emile was no exception.

Richard had watched Isabella keep her eyes focused on the ground, anywhere besides looking directly at him, unless he spoke to her within her father's presence. Then, and only then, would she look at him. Her deep brown eyes sparkled with fiery passion. Given the right environment, she would be a force to contend with.

He'd been up most of the night fighting his attraction to

her. How could a man be so attracted to a woman he barely knew? He didn't have an answer but knew if he were ever to win her affections, it would take time. Lots and lots of time.

The sails fluttered in the breeze as he fell off on his approach. "Drop anchor," he called out to his men. The rapid *ching-ching-ching* of the chains as they went through their guides in the bow was quickly followed by the splash of the anchor hitting the water.

While Isabella cleaned up the evening meal, he'd finished figuring the amount of supplies needed. Ordering the material would take a day, perhaps two.

In his brown leather satchel, he had all of his cash and the cash of the others. Truthfully, he'd been surprised at how little some of the men had given him. Many claimed they had standing credit with several of the area businesses.

Richard hollered out the orders, and the ship creaked to a halt. Isabella and Emile stood ready at the side of the ship. He waved to them and they returned the gesture.

"Ben, see the Fernandezes have a skiff to take them to shore. Mike, Pete, you two will stay on board. The rest of you can come to town with me. I'll need some hands to get these orders back to the ship. Mike, can you navigate the *Sea Dove* to the dock?"

"Yes, Sir, Captain. Ain't a woman I can't handle," he replied, his grin creasing his weather-beaten face.

"Great, watch for my signal."

Mike nodded and went back to his work. "Gentlemen, it's time; the skiff has returned."

The men worked their way over the side and down the rope ladder. At shore they jumped out of the skiff and headed up the beach. "Take her back, John. I'll send the others to relieve the three of you after we've filled our orders."

"Thanks, Captain."

Richard pulled out his list. "Let's see. Let's start with the bricks."

"Sounds good," Ben offered, and the small group made their way into town. It didn't take long before Richard had given each of the men a different task.

After a short time of searching, they found the brickyard. *"Buenos días, Señor, como está?"*

"Bien. May I help you?"

"Sí. My name is Richard Southard and I'm from Key West."

The deeply tanned man nodded.

"We've come to place an order."

"We heard the island burned up."

"We had a fire, yes. That is why we are here."

"I'd be happy to help you, Señor Southard. You have money?"

"Sí."

The man then broke into a smile. "Come to my office, Señor."

Richard soon learned in their discussion that he would only ship the bricks for which he could pay cash. The man would not extend any credit to anyone from Key West. No amount of arguing with the man could persuade him.

"Thank you, Señor. I'll need to check with the other merchants."

"Sí, I understand, Señor. But the news of the great fire has spread across the island quickly. I don't believe anyone will give credit to a man from Key West."

"Thank you, Señor." Richard nodded and headed out of the small office. "Come along, men, we've run into a problem." After a brief explanation, each man was given the task of contacting one of the businesses that had been recommended by someone on the island. The money Richard had with him was not nearly enough to satisfy the owner of the brickyard, and Richard was quickly suspecting that it would not satisfy any of the businessmen in Cuba.

"Señor Southard, I heard you were in town. I'm sorry, I cannot extend credit." The thin man with wiry gray hair looked down at the floor.

"Why? You've done business with the men on Key West before. They've always paid their bills, haven't they?"

"Sí, Señor. But how can a man pay without a business to run? Can you guarantee everyone will pay their bills within the month?"

And that was the problem. Richard could not guarantee what he did not know to be true or not true. *Lord, what am I to do?*

four

Richard paced the deck of his ship. *What should I do, Lord? Folks back home are counting on me. I've enough money to take care of my own expenses, but what about the others? Some of those businesses need to be up and running immediately for the sake of the rest of the people living on the island.*

"Señor Southard." Richard turned and saw Emile Fernandez climbing up and over the rail of the ship.

"Emile, what's the matter?" Richard hadn't expected Emile or Isabella's return until tomorrow morning.

"We have heard the merchants will not extend credit."

"Yes, it's true." Without thinking, Richard leaned over and reached his hand down for Isabella to latch on to. Her hands were strong, yet soft as delicate rose petals.

"Thank you, Mr. Southard." Isabella straightened her skirt as she stood beside her father.

Richard's gaze shifted to Emile, who was examining Richard for boldly assisting his daughter. "What are you going to do?" Emile asked.

"I'm not sure. I have some money, but it won't meet the island needs."

"No, one man shouldn't have to pay for everyone."

"No, and this man doesn't have that amount of money." Richard leaned on the rail and looked over Havana Harbor, lined with various ships of various styles and sizes. His white two-masted schooner stood out among the darker hulled ships.

"You spoke with my cousin today, sí?"

"Honestly, I don't know. I didn't catch the names of most

of the men I sought to do business with."

"My cousin, Manuel, he's short, thinly built, and has—how you say, rough, gray hair."

"Stringy?" Richard asked.

"Sí. Stringy," Emile answered, while Isabella stood quietly by her father.

"Yes, I met with a man fitting that description." He was pleasant enough but, like the rest, he would not extend credit, Richard recalled.

"Manuel, my cousin, he says he'd like to work out a deal with you."

"What kind of a deal?" Richard put his arms across his chest and braced himself.

"He says if you give him your ship, he will hold it until the money is sent from the others."

"The *Sea Dove*?" Richard's raised voice echoed off the water. "He's got to be loco."

"He may be. No one else will do business without the money. He will take your ship as, how you say, collateral?"

"Yes, collateral is the correct word." *Collateral, Lord. What would Uncle Ellis say or do? How can I tell him? "Oh, by the way, your ship is in Havana until everyone in Key West pays their bills."* Richard wagged his head from side to side. "I don't know."

Isabella reached out and touched his arm. "Manuel can be trusted, Richard."

Her rich brown eyes held his gaze. *Lord, help me. I want to believe this woman, but should I do this?* "I will need to bring this matter before the Lord. And I will need to speak further with Manuel. Can he get me all the materials on my list?"

Emile placed his hand on Richard's shoulder. "He said he would try."

Richard nodded. If ever he needed to spend time in prayer, the time was now and here, in a foreign country, all on his own to make a decision that would have a profound effect on many people. Who would fault him for not releasing his ship to the hands of such blackmail? It was ludicrous for the people of Havana to take advantage in this way. He'd been thinking of a trip up the Florida Gulf Coast or directly to Mobile as the best alternatives to this crisis. Now he was presented with an offer that could provide the necessary help but didn't give him much assurance. And, strictly speaking, he could solve his problem by buying only what he needed for himself and returning to Key West. The question was, was this a time when a man put his personal needs aside for the benefit of others?

Father God, give me wisdom, he prayed.

Late into the night, Richard continued to seek God's wisdom. He ran the what-if scenarios so often he felt they had almost become real. Deep in thought, he paced back and forth across the deck. The starry sky shimmered in its peaceful state. The gentle lull of the waves lapping the sides of the ship beat a gentle lullaby of peace. Richard closed his eyes and listened to the stillness of the world. In the distance, some night sounds from Havana played.

He pulled in a deep breath. "Lord, help me, but I see no other way. You call me to do unto others as I'd want done to me. I guess, given the same circumstance, I'd hope someone would come to my aid."

"Richard," Isabella whispered.

"Isabella?" Richard turned to see her standing in the shadows of the forward exterior wall of the captain's quarters. "What are you doing out here?"

"Looking at the moon. Are you really going to let Manuel have your ship?"

"I have no other choice."

"But you do. You don't have to accept." Isabella took a step toward him.

Richard slipped into the shadows to meet her. "A man has to do what's right, even when there appears to be great risk to himself. If I lose the *Sea Dove*, our business will suffer, compounding the damage the fire has already done."

"Then why take the risk?" she whispered.

He shouldn't continue to talk with her in secret like this. What if her father discovered them? Then again, perhaps the Lord had placed her here to help him determine the way he should go. "I don't know if I have any other choice. I've gone over the figures. There are some men in Key West that might not have the resources for months to pay off their bill to Manuel. The damage to their businesses was that extensive. Of course, I don't know their personal financial status, but I think it's safe to assume in some cases they have limited resources. For me to give up the ship would be to put a substantial amount of equity at risk."

"I understand. So why are you seriously considering doing it?" she continued to whisper.

Richard lowered his voice a tad more. "Because I believe God wants me to."

"If that be the case, Señor Southard, then you will be blessed. God will provide." She smiled and walked away.

Richard stayed in the shadows. Her honor dictated that no one know they had spoken. "Father, keep her reputation unsoiled, and thank You for her assurance that I should sacrifice the *Sea Dove*."

❧

Isabella rubbed her arms vigorously. The cool evening breeze washed over her as gooseflesh danced on her arms. She knew she shouldn't have spoken to Richard, but he seemed so lost and alone. And when she'd heard his prayer, she couldn't keep herself from speaking to him. "Lord, forgive me for being alone with him. I just wanted to help."

They had intended to sleep at her grandmother's house, but once Manuel came by and told her father about his proposal, they'd left immediately. They might be stuck on Cuba until they found passage back to Key West if Richard did give up his boat to her cousin.

Her mind drifted back to the argument her father had had with Manuel earlier in the evening. Passions flared between the men. She'd been surprised to see her father give Richard such an honorable recommendation of his cousin. But that was the custom. Families were honest and open with each other—but only with family. It wasn't that her father didn't trust his cousin, Manuel. He was just angered that a man who had worked well with others in previous days would be so concerned about extending the credit at this time.

If there was one thing Isabella understood, it was finances. Working mathematical figures in her head was a talent she possessed and one her father worked to keep well hidden. Many men felt women just didn't have an aptitude for numbers.

Isabella unfastened her skirt and slipped it over the chair so it would be fresh in the morning. She hadn't packed enough clothes for an extended stay. How would they get home and when?

She removed the rest of her clothing and slipped on her nightclothes. Before sliding under the covers, she went to Richard's desk and looked over the figures he'd been working with earlier in the day. Her hands trembled as she realized the amount of money Richard would be sacrificing for others. "Oh, Lord, keep Manuel honest." She let the paper float back to the desk.

Isabella jumped from the gentle knock on the door. "Isabella, it's Richard, are you in there?"

"Yes. Did you need something from your desk?" She spoke behind the closed door, her hand braced against the door, her heart pounding.

"No, it can wait until morning."

Isabella heard her father's voice. "Señor Southard, may I help you?"

Isabella's face grew hot. Her father wouldn't understand. . . .

"Isabella?"

"Sí, Papá, I'm fine." She ran to the bed and slipped under the covers.

"Emile, tell me more about Manuel," she heard Richard say. Her father answered, and the two men's voices receded from the door.

Isabella clutched the covers to her chest. She'd disobeyed her parents tonight by seeking out Richard. To have her father discover her talking with him. . . Thankfully the door was closed, not that she would have opened it. "Lord, I care for this man far too much. Mother will see it in my eyes when I return. Help me, Lord. I don't want my heart to go to anyone who isn't the best You have for me."

⁂

The next morning Richard woke still upbraiding himself for having been so foolish as to approach the captain's quarters. Emile's fatherly reprimand consisted of a look that would send any sane man running as far away from Isabella Fernandez as he could possibly get. And yet, he found himself even more attracted to her.

Cold ham and biscuits sat heavy in his stomach, a sharp contrast to Isabella's fine cooking the day before. He'd assembled the men early this morning and asked them to gather any of their personal effects on the ship, as well as anything others might have left on board. For some reason, he knew he had to give the *Sea Dove* as a sign of good faith, but he also had the nagging suspicion he might never see the ship again. Richard rubbed his temples and went back to his paperwork, checking and rechecking his figures.

How is it that a man can know what is the right thing to do and yet still have the hardest time trusting it is the best thing? Richard kneaded the tension out of his neck.

"Señor Southard."

Richard found Isabella standing outside the cabin. "Isabella." What could he say? He looked past her to see her father was nowhere in sight.

"I saw your figures last night. I just wanted to say, you've been asked to sacrifice a lot. And thank you for understanding our customs."

"Why are you here now, Isabella? If your father caught you, he'd be very angry." Richard stood up at the desk and assembled his paperwork.

"Sí, he would. But I'm out here keeping my distance."

"But you're still speaking with me." Richard slung the leather pouch with his papers and money over his shoulder. He stepped closer to the door. "You know as well as I, your father would not approve."

"True, but I have come to retrieve my belongings. My father can't object to that."

"No, I suppose he can't. Come in."

Isabella stood steadfast outside the cabin. "No, I'll wait until you're through."

"So, if I stay in here and continue to talk with you, your father would not object?" He knew the answer before he asked, but the thought of sneaking a brief conversation with Isabella controlled his better judgment.

"No, he would object. Richard, are your figures correct? Would you be sacrificing thirty-five thousand dollars?"

"Yes. But how did you come up with that? I never put the figure down."

"I'm fairly good with mathematics."

"Ah, Nanna is very good with figures too. She taught me well." Richard opened his hidden panel and pulled out an additional leather pouch.

"What is that?"

"Isabella, has anyone ever told you, you ask too many questions?"

Her brown eyes shimmered. "Some have said as much."

Richard chuckled. "You are an amazing woman, Isabella. Now if you'll excuse me, I need to see your cousin and make arrangements."

She stepped aside for him to pass.

"Richard," she whispered.

He turned to look at her. Her head bowed down. "You're an amazing man," she whispered.

Richard forced every muscle in his body not to reach out and pull her toward him. He'd never met a woman to whom he'd been so attracted. Yes, she was beautiful, but that wasn't the only source of attraction. Every stolen moment together he'd learned another fascinating feature about her. She definitely piqued his interest. A change in subject would help. "Can you and your father afford passage back to Key West?"

"Father will find a way."

"I'm sorry, Isabella; this hasn't been a pleasant trip for you."

She looked at him then. "It is not your fault, Richard."

Richard. She'd said it again. For a young Hispanic woman, she was very daring. To speak to him, to call him by his first name, to understand math. . . Perhaps, he should seek her father's permission to court Isabella. *But if I did, Emile might think that something had already happened between Isabella and me.*

Has it, Lord?

five

"Papá, I did not tell Señor Southard." Isabella stood defending herself in her grandmother's small home. Thankfully, her grandmother was working in the garden. She could just imagine the scorn she would get from her grandmother for having spoken with Richard Southard.

"Then how did he know?" Confusion and anger played across her father's face.

"Did you pay him for passage to Cuba?"

"No, I offered, but he refused."

"He knows on his own. I swear I did not tell him we didn't have the money to buy passage on another ship."

Isabella rehearsed what she did tell Richard in her mind. Not once did she mention that the money would be a problem. Part of her father's anger with Manuel was that his plan had put them in a difficult place to return to Key West, and Manuel had not offered to help.

Emile paced back and forth in the small front room. Isabella focused on a small table he had refurbished for her grandmother. "We will have to pay Señor Southard back."

"Sí, I'm sure he would agree." Isabella thought again about the tremendous sacrifice Richard was making for the folks in Key West. Would anyone ever really know the extent of his benevolence?

"Papá, we must go now. Señor Southard's instructions said the ship would be leaving very soon."

"Sí." Emile grabbed his bag, kissed his mother as she entered the house, and headed for the door.

"Grandma, I love you. *Adíos.*" Isabella hugged the frail woman. Her father had tried to convince his mother to come to Key West and live with them, but she refused. "This is my home," was her reply.

Isabella and her father hurried through Havana's narrow streets, making their way to the harbor. Isabella looked for Richard Southard but could not find him. She couldn't find him on the ship, either. He'd purchased passage for them in a large guest room of the captain's. The ship was a four-masted schooner, much larger than Richard Southard's.

"Captain, is Señor Southard on this vessel?"

"No, Miss Fernandez. Mr. Southard had more business in Havana."

"Gracías."

Isabella found the voyage uneventful, boring almost. Thoughts of Richard Southard and the *Sea Dove* seemed more pressing. Admittedly, it wasn't as grand of a ship, a work boat, Richard had called it. But somehow this four-masted schooner with all its glamour and wealthy guests seemed to pale in comparison.

❧

Back in Key West, Isabella tried to find a job. Day after day no employment could be found. If she were a man, there would be plenty of work. But as a woman, there was nothing. Richard had returned to Key West on a cargo ship loaded with most of the materials the islanders had ordered. Some spoke of his having to leave the *Sea Dove* in Havana as collateral, but the urgency of rebuilding the island kept the people from their usual gossip.

Every day she would walk past Richard Southard's property, and every day she was careful not to speak with him. Today, she hesitated as she gazed over the ruins of the Southard warehouse.

"Looks pretty bad," a voice said from behind.

Isabella gasped. "Don't scare me like that."

"I'm sorry," Richard apologized. "I thought you would have heard me coming."

"Any word about your ship?" She turned to face him.

"Nothing worth mentioning. There are several who will not be able to pay their debt for at least sixty days."

"Oh, Richard, I'm so sorry. What are you going to do?" Isabella fought the desire to touch him.

"I'm going to do what my uncle used to do. I purchased enough wood to rebuild the dock. I have the men sponging now, and we'll wash and dry the sponges on the dock. I'll barter with every captain who comes to port to haul the sponges. Slowly, we'll get some more money in and I'll be able to purchase the material for the building, unless the others can pay me back sooner."

Isabella scanned the nearly completed rebuilt dock. "You've worked quickly."

"Mo's been a tremendous help. As you can see, we've only rebuilt about half of it. I hope to have the rest of it built by the end of the week, depending upon the manpower that's available."

Yes, plenty of work for men, nothing for a woman.

"Isabella?" Richard perused the area, then settled his gaze back on her. "Is something wrong?"

"What? No. No, nothing."

"You seemed to have drifted far away there for a minute."

"I've been trying to find work, but there's only work for men in Key West right now."

"Oh, I'm sorry. I'm afraid I don't have work for a woman, either."

Isabella felt a crimson blush working its way up her neck. She hadn't meant to hint that he. . . "I didn't mean to imply that you should hire me. I know your company has no place for a woman."

"I will pray for you to find a suitable job. What do you do?"

"Nothing. I mean, I could do plenty, but no one will hire me. I tried to get hired in the banks, but no one trusts a woman to handle money."

"Hmm."

"I've tried to get work at the baker's, but he's not hiring. Let's face it, I've tried to find work everywhere, but no one is hiring women. Everyone's too involved with getting the town rebuilt. Not that I blame them, but. . ."

"It would be nice to be employed."

"Exactly." He understood and was not offended. Why was it so easy to speak with him?

Richard sat down on the dock. Isabella started to follow suit, then stopped herself.

Richard jumped up. He'd seen her hesitation. "I'm sorry. I forgot."

She wished she could forget. If it weren't for the large Hispanic population and the fact that everyone on Key West knew her father, she would have loved to sit down beside him to talk, just talk. *What is the harm in that, Lord?*

❧

Richard cleared his throat. He'd felt so comfortable talking with her. "Isabella?"

"Sí," she whispered.

"Isabella!" Emile Fernandez roared. Richard would recognize the man's voice anywhere.

"Over here, Papá."

"Señor Southard," Emile said curtly.

"Buenos días, Señor Fernandez, como está?"

"Bien." Emile's voice was curt. "Isabella, why are you here?"

"I was on my way back home."

Richard watched as Isabella's gaze caught her father's. She would be in trouble. Richard knew he had to come up with something. "Emile, your daughter is good with numbers, right?"

"Sí, Señor, she has a pretty face but a very keen mind."

Richard wouldn't acknowledge the part about her pretty face, but the mind was neutral territory, he hoped. "Emile, would it be all right with you if I asked your daughter to come and work for me?"

"Pardon?"

"I could use someone to work on my financial records. I'm afraid with all the work I've been doing on the dock, and eventually the building, I haven't time to keep my books. Uncle Ellis would not be pleased. If Isabella feels she could learn the bookkeeping, would you give her your permission to come and work for me?"

"You have no office. Where would she work?" Emile's confusion deepened.

"I have an office at my home. Cook is there most days. I would be here on the dock most of the day. However, I would need to talk with Miss Isabella on occasions in order to conduct business." *Why am I doing this? I don't need a bookkeeper that badly. Admit it, Richard, when it comes to a certain Miss Isabella Fernandez, you do some mighty foolish things. Like paying for her transport back to Key West on a luxury ship while you yourself were snuggled up with the building supplies you were bringing back to the island.*

"It is not proper for a young woman to talk with a young man without a chaperone."

"Papá," Isabella pleaded.

Emile raised his hand in objection. Isabella stood rigid and clutched her hands into fists. Richard could tell she was fighting to obey her father, while her heart rebelled against being treated like a child.

"Yes, but I would be her employer. Isn't that allowed?" *Employers do have to talk with employees,* he reasoned. "And as I said, Cook will be there. I will try to always speak to Isabella when Cook is in earshot. Would that be acceptable?"

"How do you know Isabella has a mind for math?"

Richard swallowed the lump forming in his throat. Emile had him there. "She commented about some figures I had been working on in Havana. Only a skilled person would have come to the right tabulation."

"And how do you know this?" Emile stared at his daughter.

"Papá, Señor Southard behaved properly. He was in his quarters, and I commented from outside the room while we were on board the ship."

Emile turned toward his daughter. He was about to speak to Isabella in Spanish when he stopped himself, Richard guessed. Emile knew that was hopeless since Richard understood the language.

"This does not please me." Emile didn't break his gaze from Isabella.

"Señor Fernandez, would you agree that Isabella needs a job?"

"Sí."

"And would you also agree that your daughter does not have a mind that should be limited to simple tasks such as someone's laundry?"

"Sí." Emile sighed.

"Then let me hire your daughter. I give you my word, I will not behave in an inappropriate manner with her."

"Your honor?"

Richard swallowed hard. He'd been taught his word was his bond. Could he honestly live up to this commitment, especially in light of the fact that he and Isabella had already spoken on two, no, three occasions? "Sí, Señor."

"Then she will work for you. When should she begin?"

Isabella smiled and turned her head away from her father's gaze.

If she was as interested in him as he was in her, Richard knew he would have a problem on his hands in future days. *Do not fret about tomorrow. . . .* "She can begin tomorrow. Come to my home around nine o'clock."

He'd have to rearrange his schedule and work on the books tonight. They were in sad shape, not only from the past week because of the fire, but he'd been putting off the bookwork for about a month. He'd been thinking too much about himself and his future to do all that was needed for the business.

"Nine," Emile repeated. "She'll be there. *Gracías,* Señor Southard. I know you are a man of honor and you will treat my daughter with proper respect."

Richard nodded, his throat too tight to speak.

As Emile escorted Isabella away from Richard, she turned and mouthed a silent thank-you. His heart soared. She appreciated the job. She was independent enough to want to have found one on her own, but respectful enough to allow her father the final decision.

"Lord, You're going to have to help me here. Working side by side with Isabella will test my strength in more ways than one. She's so beautiful, Lord. But You know that."

Richard bent down and pulled out a charred stick from the rubble. "Can I really rebuild this business?" He'd sent letters to the companies expecting shipments, telling them of the fire and an approximate date they could expect delivery. Now the only question was, could he come through?

∂∘

As soon as they entered their home, Isabella regained a measure of composure. "Papá, you embarrassed me in front of Señor Southard."

"Me? What about you, Daughter? Speaking to a man alone, what were you thinking? Do you want everyone to speak of you as being a. . .a. . ."

"Papá, people speak to each other all the time on the island. No one thinks that way anymore. In Cuba, yes. Here, no."

"There are still plenty of our people living here in Key West. They think as I," Emile insisted, folding his arms across his chest.

Her mother walked into the room. "What has Isabella done now?" she asked, rubbing her hands on a dishcloth.

"She was speaking with a young man."

Yolanda turned and faced Isabella. "Who?"

Isabella couldn't face her mother's examination and glanced at the floor. "Señor Southard."

"I see. Emile, what did you do?"

"I contained myself. Richard Southard speaks our language, so I could not speak to Isabella without him understanding everything I said. She is, however, going to work for him."

"Pardon?"

"Now, now, relax, Yolanda. I have it all arranged. She'll be working at his office in his house while he's working on the docks. There will be a time or two when he needs to speak with her, but Cook will be in the house."

Yolanda lifted her daughter's chin. "Do you want to work for Señor Southard?"

"Sí, Mima, very much."

Her mother's gaze fixed on Isabella's. "We shall speak later."

"All right. I'm going to my room; excuse me." Isabella stepped back and made her way down the hall, leaving her parents speaking in rapid whispers. How could she keep herself from speaking with Richard Southard? He was so comfortable to talk with. He was a man of honor; perhaps she could depend upon him to keep their relationship purely innocent.

"Hah," Isabella taunted her reflection in the mirror. Richard Southard was as attracted to her as she was to him; she'd seen it in his blue-gray eyes. She removed the pins from her hair and picked up her hairbrush.

She had a job, a real job. One that fit her talents and abilities. She smiled at herself as she worked her hair with the brush, then began to pace in the small path between her bed and the wall.

"Lord, thank You for the job. But can Richard Southard afford to hire me at this time? I saw the figures he worked on in Havana. The risk he was taking, the loan he was making to others—how can he afford it?"

"Isabella, it is not for us to question." Yolanda walked in

and sat down on Isabella's bed. "Come, sit with me."

Isabella's hands shook. She folded them on her lap.

"You care for Señor Southard, don't you?" Her mother spoke in loving Spanish.

"Sí."

"Does your papá know?"

"No."

"Does Señor Southard know?"

"No. . .I don't know."

"I see." Yolanda reached over and held her daughter's hand. "It's hard to be a woman and respect our ways. It is harder for you having grown up in Key West and not Cuba. But you have to understand how your papá and I feel about such matters."

"Oh, Mima, I do, honest I do. It's just that when I'm near Richard—"

"Richard?"

"Señor Southard."

"I know his name, Darling. I'm surprised you feel comfortable calling him by his given name."

Isabella took in a deep breath. "I know, Mima, I'm surprised at myself too. But that is just it. I feel this connection with this man. He's so incredibly handsome and—"

Yolanda whispered a laugh. "And you expect to be able to keep your mind on your work for him?"

"I will work, and I will do a good job," Isabella affirmed with ardent determination. "I will try not to speak with him unless it relates to our work."

"And what will you do if Richard asks to kiss you?"

Love every minute of it. The heat of embarrassment warmed her cheeks. "Señor Southard would not do that." Oh, but she hoped he would.

"I see, and why do you say that?"

"Because he gave Papá his word."

"What exactly did he promise in his word?"

"That he would not dishonor me."

"I see." Her mother caressed her hand. "Isabella, promise me something."

"What, Mima?"

"Promise me that when these feelings for Señor Southard develop to a point when you think you'll burst inside, that you will tell me." Yolanda pushed Isabella's wayward hair behind her shoulders.

Could she do that? Were her thoughts already to that point? No, she wasn't about to explode. . . . "Sí, Mima, I will do that."

"Good, because at that time we will have to speak to your father about your marriage to Richard Southard."

"Marriage? Mima, I'm not going to work for Señor Southard just to marry him."

"No? Then why are you going to work for him?"

six

Richard pinched the bridge of his nose after running his fingers across his eyelids. It was nearly midnight and he was still working on the paperwork.

"Richard, what are you doing up so late?" Cook placed her hands on her ample hips.

The sound of her voice sent a sense of peace washing over him. "Working?"

"Whatever for? Didn't ya say you hired Isabella Fernandez to do this work?"

"Yes, but I need to get the books in order before she starts."

"Seems to me she could be doing that. You just need to show her how and let her go to work."

Richard scanned the various ledger sheets. "You might be right, Cook." He tapped the paper covered with scribbles.

"Richie, you told me what happened in Cuba about the ship. But what is goin' on with you and Isabella?" She sat down on a high-backed chair by the door, her voice filled with motherly concern.

"Nothing, really. She needed a job, I know she has the mind for the figures, and I'm behind."

"So, ya don't have feelings for her?" Her gray eyebrows rose into her warm, cocoa forehead.

"Cook," Richard sighed, "she's special, and she's attractive, but I don't have time for romance. I have too much to do, too much to make right before James returns to take his place in the family business."

"So is that what's been on your mind the past few weeks? James?"

"Somewhat. The past week I haven't given it much thought

other than the fact that I need to get the business back on its feet and I have a limited amount of time in which to do it." Richard pushed his chair back away from his desk.

"Care for a game a checkers?" Cook winked.

Richard chuckled. When he was a small boy, it had been his favorite game. "Don't you think we should retire for the evening?"

"Sure, but one game won't hurt ya, unless you think you're going to lose."

"You're on. I'll fix us a cup a tea; you set up the board. Would you prefer chess?" he asked, heading toward the kitchen.

"Goodness, no, Child. That takes far more brain power than what I have at this hour."

A game of checkers proved to be the distraction he needed, although it lasted longer than he thought it would. Either he'd gotten rusty or Cook had been practicing.

"Good game, Richie. Now, I think I should retire." Cook rose slowly from the chair.

"You and me both. Morning comes early when you stay up this late. Go to bed, Cook. I'll clean up."

Richard straightened the sitting room and put their cups into the sink. Once Cook would have flatly refused his offer to help. She definitely was getting older. The fact that she had already lived longer than most didn't make it easier to accept the prospect that she might be gone one day. What would he do? He'd experienced losses in his life—his mother, his father—but those events happened when he was so young. "Lord, keep her around a bit longer and keep her healthy." He rinsed the teacups and headed up the stairs to his bedroom.

Dressed for bed, he settled between the sheets after completing his prayers. The lily of the ruins drifted into his mind as he floated off to sleep.

❧

"Richie, wake up." Cook placed a loving hand across his

brow. "Son, are you feelin' all right?"

His eyes flickered open. "Cook?"

"It's well past dawn and you hadn't surfaced, so I thought I better check on you. Are you all right?"

Richard did a hazy check of his senses and determined he felt all right. "I'm fine, just overslept."

"We were up rather late last night," she said with a wink.

"Yes, we were. What time is it?"

"Just about nine. Isn't that the time you said Isabella Fernandez was comin' over this mornin'?"

Richard bolted up out of bed. "Yes. Where are my trousers?"

"Over the chair. I picked them up off the floor."

"Oh, sorry. I guess I was really tired when I went to bed."

"Uh-huh. You get yourself ready; I'll fix ya some breakfast."

"Thanks. If Isabella comes before I'm dressed, sit her in the front room, please."

"Certainly."

Richard poured some water into the basin and washed his face and brushed his teeth. "I can't believe I overslept, Lord." *Admit it, you were having pleasant dreams of Isabella.*

He heard Isabella's voice. "Good morning, Cook."

"Mornin', Miz Fernandez. Mr. Southard will be with you shortly. Can I get ya a cup a tea?"

"No, thank you."

"Come this way." Richard glimpsed Cook walking her into the sitting room from the top of the stairs. He slowed his pace. He didn't need to appear as if he were in a rush. The question was, was he rushing because he'd woken up late or because Isabella was in his house? Truthfully, it was probably the latter, he admitted.

Richard took the steps one at a time, slowly descending to give himself time to catch his breath and calm his nerves. He'd promised her father he would be a man of honor. "Lord, give me strength," he whispered before entering the front sitting room. "Good morning, Miss Fernandez."

"Good morning, Señor Southard." Isabella rose from the sofa.

"Sit, sit, I will be with you in a couple of minutes." He turned to Cook. "Can I bring you something from the kitchen?"

"No, Sir, I'm fine." Cook sat with her feet up on the footrest. Seeing her resting like that sent a flicker of worry through his heart.

"Excuse me, ladies."

❧

Isabella couldn't believe the complexity of Richard Southard's financial records. Not only was he tracking the monies from the sponging business, but he also had his own personal finances that he had invested in various businesses in the North. On paper, Richard Southard was a very wealthy man. At the moment, his cash flow was more than most, but the employee salaries would quickly deplete the limited funds. He'd need an infusion of revenue before the month was up, she analyzed.

They'd spent the morning with him showing her the various ledgers and accounts. What had surprised her even more was the total outlay of cash he'd added to the debt for the fire. She had no idea he'd brought that much money with him to Cuba, and she doubted anyone else on the island knew just how deep his sacrifice had been.

Richard did not return to the house by the end of the day. "Cook, I'll be leaving now. I've left a note for Mr. Southard on his desk. Would you see that he gets it?"

"Of course, Child. Did you enjoy the work?"

"Yes, very much. I'm not sure what he'll want me to work on tomorrow, so that's what I asked him in my note."

"I'm sure Richie will have more work for you."

Isabella nodded. Why did people still insist on calling him Richie? "Good night, Cook."

"Good night. I'll see you in the morning."

Isabella walked down the streets and worked her way

toward her family home. It felt good to have a job. And yet, at the same time, she found herself even more drawn to Richard Southard. She never would have guessed he had so much wealth. He and his uncle's family lived a conservative lifestyle on Key West. They weren't in the largest home on the island. They didn't go to all the elite social occasions, as best she knew. Not that she or her family went to such events. Her father's job of rolling cigars was not a position that would bring wealth into a household, yet her parents had always managed to feed and clothe the family.

"Papá, Mima, I'm home."

&

The next week began and ended the same. She'd go off to work, put in a full day, and come home to help with the evening meal. She was more and more comfortable with the Southards' books. Several of the businessmen had sent along notes to say when they could pay their debt in Cuba, and a few of the island men had paid some or part of what they owed Richard. He never commented on it. He simply gave her the receipts for the day and told her what was what and where to file the information.

As the days passed, she found her father's worries about her being in a compromising situation unfounded. Richard left notes; she left notes; they were hardly ever in the same room together.

As she was thinking about Richard, Isabella opened a piece of his correspondence and scanned it. "Oh, no."

She got up and ran from the desk. "Cook," she hollered.

"What's the matter, Miz?"

"Is Richard at the docks?"

"I believe so, but I don't keep track of the boy any longer."

"If he should come home, tell him I went to town to look for him at his dock."

"What's the trouble?"

"Later, Cook. It's important."

Isabella ran out of the house and hurried down to the wharf. "Richard," she called. "Richard!" she called again. No one was there. What should she do now?

&

"Richard Southard?" Marc Dabney called after him. "Hold on a minute."

Richard turned around. Marc's rounded belly and balding head showed his age. "What can I do for you, Mr. Dabney?"

"Nothing. It's more of what I can do for you."

"What's that?"

"I heard they are holding your ship in Havana as collateral until the residents pay off their debts."

Richard nodded. It wasn't something he wanted spread around the island, but information of this sort was readily shared. "Yes."

"I'm willing to loan you enough to return your vessel."

"Why would you do this?"

Marc grinned. "Call it my generous nature. I can see that you weren't able to buy the materials to rebuild your warehouse."

"I can put that off for awhile."

"The choice is yours. If you'd like the monies, I'd be happy to lend it."

"Lend, as in provide a loan for a certain interest rate?"

Marc reached over and placed his hand on Richard's shoulder. "Minimal profit."

"What percentage rate are we talking, Mr. Dabney?"

"Call me Marc."

"Marc," Richard repeated with a nod of his head.

"I'm thinking ten percent. We could negotiate on that point. It would all depend on the amount of time you'd need the money."

"Put it in writing and I'll give it consideration." What else could he say? He might need to take this loan in order to make payroll.

"Have a good evening. I'll get the proposal put together

and have it delivered to your. . . Where would you like to have me deliver the paperwork?"

"My home."

Marc Dabney nodded and waddled down the street.

There had to be a better way. Richard sighed.

A ship had come in from Cuba with a fresh supply of beef today, and he wanted to pick some up for dinner. He headed toward the market, grateful it was still standing.

"Richard."

Richard turned to see Micah coming toward him. "I'm glad I caught up with you. Mo said I'd find you in town."

"What's the matter, Micah?"

"Nothing. My father and I were just talking about your ship being held in Cuba and we wanted to offer you some room on our next ship leaving port—and any others—until you have the *Sea Dove* back."

Richard extended his hand. "Thank you, Micah, I appreciate that. I can't dry as many sponges at the moment, but I do have a shipment that should be ready in a couple of days."

"Excellent. I'll have our skipper come by your dock after he's loaded our supplies. Oh, this ship is heading north. I didn't figure you wanted a shipment going to South America," Micah added.

"No, I don't have any customers down there."

"Heading to the market?" Micah asked with a glint of excitement in his eyes.

"Yup."

"Me too. Fresh beef is more common than when I first moved here, but it still comes in limited quantities."

"That's one thing I miss about living in New York. I had fresh meat regularly, even raised a couple heads for myself and the neighbors. Pigs were easy and less maintenance."

"Don't have that kind of land down here," Micah commented, keeping in step. A line was forming outside the butcher's.

"My farm back home is ten times larger than the entire island and has hardly any people there."

"Do you miss it?"

"Yes and no. I'm uncertain. I like Key West. I grew up here. But there was something very satisfying about working the land. I suspect it's something from my father. Uncle Ellis said his brother loved the land and was a natural farmer."

"Few stay here for long," Micah observed and raked his golden brown hair with his right hand.

"Yeah, I'm wondering what effect it will have on my uncle and his family living back in the old house, working the land. There's a part of me that could just walk away from the sponge business since it went up in flames but another part of me that needs to rebuild. It will be James's one day."

"Is that what James would want?"

"Honestly, I don't know. But it's not my choice to make. It's something he has to decide for himself. I'm responsible to have something left here for him to choose."

"You know my grandfather prearranged my father's career. Dad gave me the option and I still chose to go in the family business. Is your uncle forcing James?"

"Oh, no, not at all. It's part of the reason he brought the family back North, to give the boys the options and show them there is another way of life." Not to mention Richard hadn't been sure if he wanted to sell the property or keep working the land. The next couple years in Key West were to give him that time to decide.

"My father and I have been having the same discussion. With the railroad's expansion, Key West seems an unnecessary port for shipping cotton. Savannah and Mobile are better locations. I met my wife here and our children were born here, though. It could be a tough adjustment moving to either place. My preference would be to go back to Savannah rather than Mobile."

Richard grinned. "Savannah is a beautiful city—been there a few times."

The line moved forward a couple of steps.

Richard lowered his voice and continued their conversation. "Marc Dabney just made me an interesting offer."

"Oh, what was that?"

"He offered to lay out the funds to get my boat back from Havana."

"Interesting." Micah leaned in closer and lowered his voice a fraction more. "Are you inclined to take him up on it?"

"I'll have to do some calculating. For instance, is the interest he'll charge less than the loss of not having the boat?"

"You've got your work cut out for you. Say, that reminds me. I heard Isabella Fernandez has been doing some book-keeping for you."

"You heard correctly. She's got quite a head for numbers."

Micah stepped inside the threshold of the building. Richard wasn't too surprised that there were half a dozen folks still in front of them in line.

"Do you have enough work to keep Miss Fernandez employed full time?"

"I do at the moment, but it's quite possible that soon I won't have need of full time help until I have the warehouse rebuilt."

"If she can hold her own with the figures, I might have some part-time work for her also."

"I'll keep it in mind if I have to reduce her hours. She's so efficient I might just run out of work for her."

Micah stood up to the counter. "A four-pound roast, please."

Richard watched as the butcher cut a large hunk of meat for Micah and his family. A steak had been what Richard had wanted, but looking at the roast, he wondered if he should reconsider. His mouth watered in anticipation of a feast.

"Richard," Micah leaned into him and whispered. "Be careful around Marc Dabney."

seven

Isabella hurried back to the house. Richard was nowhere to be found. She'd have to leave a message for him to read the correspondence she'd opened. *Cook will bring it to his attention right away,* she reasoned.

In the office, she penned a note, folded it, and placed it on top of the opened letter. "Cook," Isabella called as she headed toward the kitchen. "Cook?" she searched further and headed into the kitchen. The older woman sat on the floor. "What's the matter?"

"I. . .I'm. . ." Cook struggled for the words.

"Shh, can I help you to your bed? To a chair?"

"Doc. . ." The old black woman fell back against the floor.

"Help me, Lord! Help her." Isabella jumped up and ran to the living room. She pulled a small pillow from the sofa and a lap blanket. Back in the kitchen, she placed the blanket over Cook and gently placed her head on the pillow. "I'll get the doctor. Hang on, Cook."

Cook blinked her eyes but did not speak.

"Dear Jesus, be with her." Isabella raced down Front Street toward the center of town.

"Isabella?" Richard hollered from across the street.

"Richard, Cook's ill, she's on the floor in the kitchen."

"I'll get Doctor Miller. Go back and stay with her."

"All right." Isabella turned and hightailed it back to the house. Should she go get Lizzy? Someone should, but someone needed to be with Cook also. Who should she ask? Who was around? Just at that moment Peg Bower stepped out of Vivian Matlin's old house.

Isabella called out, "Mrs. Bower, would you go get Lizzy

Greene? Cook's fallen ill."

"I'll go get her," Peg said, waving to her to go on. "Tell Cook I'm praying for her."

Isabella continued to speed through the Southards' yard and into the kitchen. *Lord, tell me what to do.*

"Cook, the doctor's on his way."

Isabella knelt by the fallen woman. Her eyes seemed dim. Isabella reached for Cook's hand and held it. "Cook, answer me, please." Tears pooled, threatening to spill onto her cheeks. She didn't know Cook well, but during the past couple of weeks, she'd come to care deeply for her. She seemed so vibrant. What could have happened to her?

"Cook, Isabella!" Richard hollered. "Where are you?"

"The kitchen."

"Cook, speak to me." Richard bent down and let the tears stream down his face.

Isabella choked back her own. He loved this woman, truly loved her.

"Isabella, help me. I'm going to put her in her bed."

"What can I do?"

"When I lay her down, you can make her comfortable."

"Sí."

Richard hoisted the woman and carried her back to her room. "Hang on, Cook, the doctor will be here in just a couple of minutes."

He turned to Isabella. "What happened?"

"I don't know. I came into the kitchen to give her a message for you and found her holding her chest, sitting on the floor. She didn't speak."

Lizzie rushed through the door and knelt beside the bed. "Momma!"

Lizzy, unlike her mother, had kept her slim figure even after seven children. But Lizzy was now a grandmother, and the white in her well-groomed hair gave her an air of quiet sophistication.

Isabella stood back. Lizzy would care for her mother's needs.

Richard bent over Cook and kissed her cheek. "I love you." His eyes were red with tears.

Doctor Miller came running in with his black leather bag. "What happened?"

Isabella explained what she'd seen.

"Did she hold her arm?"

"Not that I noticed."

"Thank you. Now, if all of you will excuse me while I examine my patient."

"I'd like to stay," Lizzy asked.

"Yes, Lizzy, you can help. The rest of you can leave."

They left Cook's bedroom, and Isabella followed Richard back to the kitchen. He continued out the door into the backyard. Should she follow him? Or did he want to be alone?

Isabella stayed in the kitchen, picked up the blanket and pillow, and returned them to the sitting room. *Sometimes a person just needs to be alone,* she reasoned.

ঝ

Richard escaped into the trees' shadows in the back garden. He fell to his knees. "Father God, please don't take her now. I need her. I'm not ready to let her go just yet. I know it's horribly selfish, but she means the world to me. If it's at all possible, please let her stay a bit longer."

Salty tears stung his cheeks. Impatiently, he wiped them away. *A full-grown man and I'm crying like a four year old.*

"Oh, God, please don't take her." He crumpled over in his anguish. "I know she isn't my grandmother, but she certainly is as close as I've ever had to one." His father's parents had died before he was four. His mother's parents had visited a couple of times after he went to live in Key West with his uncle, but they passed on before he'd moved north.

He continued to pour his heart out to God for what seemed like an eternity. Finally, it occurred to him that he should go back in and see what the doctor had to say.

He felt someone gently place a hand on his shoulder. "Richard," Isabella whispered. "Here, place this on your eyes. It will help."

She held out a damp cloth. Richard took it and did as she recommended. She sat down on the ground beside him. "You love her a lot, don't you?"

"Yes, she's lived in my house since I was four. Before Uncle Ellis married Nanna. I've been noticing how much she's slowed down, but I wasn't prepared for this."

"She loves the Lord, Richard."

"Is that supposed to make it all better?" he cut back.

"No, but it helps, doesn't it? Knowing that even if she does. . .well, if she does, you know. . .she'll be going to heaven."

"Yeah, I suppose that does help some. There are just so many different things going on right now that I. . .I. . ." What did he really want? Was his personal need for Cook in his life his only reason for wanting her around? She wouldn't mind going to heaven. She'd been looking forward to it for years. But Cook always reasoned the good Lord kept her around for a reason. Sometimes she'd say she had to keep busy "messin' with people's lives so as they get it right." And that she would. Cook had no trouble telling folks how things really were.

"I guess it's selfish, really. I love her, and she's a stabilizing force in my life. Not having my family with me right now, it's given me solace knowing she was here."

Isabella placed her hand on top of his. "I think I understand that."

Richard looked at her rich chocolate eyes, her high cheekbones, and her silky golden skin, and he wanted to reach out and kiss her. He pushed back her hair and cupped the back of her neck. He gave it the slightest pressure, feeling her body shiver from his touch. "Oh, Isabella, I—"

"Don't, don't say it, Richard. We can't."

Richard shook his head. "I'm sorry." How stupid could he be? Her father would be furious. He'd given his word he wouldn't act in an improper way toward Isabella, and here he was about to kiss her senseless. But she wanted him to. Regret gathered in her eyes.

"I'm sorry, Isabella. It won't happen again."

"But. . ."

"No, Isabella, I need you to work for me. I can't ruin that by allowing my emotions to take control. If I kissed you, your father would never permit you to come and work for me again."

"Unless you married me."

Marriage, for a kiss? No, thank you. "I think we'd better go back inside and see what the doctor has to say."

He got up and extended a hand to Isabella. She refused it, which was probably a good thing. Having that woman's hand in his own would only stir up more desires, desires he couldn't act upon.

"After I find out what the doctor has said about Cook, I'm going home. My parents will be wondering where I am."

Richard nodded. What could he say? He'd taken a private moment and turned it into something they both regretted.

Inside the house, they found Lizzy and the doctor sitting at the kitchen table. "How is she, Dr. Miller?" Richard asked, taking a seat in one of the remaining chairs.

"Her heart is failing."

Richard's own felt like it could burst. "Is she. . . ?"

"She'll be around for a little while if she takes it easy."

Lizzy wiped her tears with a linen napkin. Richard reached out and held her hand. "She's resting now," she said. "I'm going to stay with her, if you don't mind, Richard." Lizzy's voice cracked.

"Of course I don't mind. You know you're more than welcome any time in this home." He squeezed her hand.

"Thanks."

Isabella stood in the doorway. "Mrs. Greene, my family and I will be praying."

"Thank you, Isabella."

"Señor Southard, I'll be back in the morning."

"Señor" again; it was probably best. "Buenos noches, Isabella." Richard turned back to the doctor. "What can we do to help Cook, Doctor?"

≈

Isabella fought her tears the entire walk home. As she suspected, her parents were getting ready to look for her. The thought of them coming upon her and Richard when he was about to kiss her. . . Thank the good Lord that didn't happen.

"Isabella, what's wrong?"

"Cook has taken ill. The doctor says her heart is failing."

"Oh no, we must pray for her." Yolanda's words quieted Isabella's heart.

"Sí, I told Miss Lizzy we would pray. It's all so sad; she's such a wonderful woman."

"Ah, but each person is given a time to live and a time to die." Her father spoke softly.

"I know, but it doesn't make it easier." Truth was, her tears were not just for Cook—she truly would miss the woman— but her tears were more for herself and Richard and what probably would never happen between them due to her family's ancient traditions. Life could be so unfair sometimes. "I'm not hungry tonight. If you don't mind, I'd like some time alone in my room."

"Sí, you do what you need to do, *Niña*." Her mother gave her a tender embrace and Isabella slipped past her. Her room was filled with familiar memories, items from her entire life, a short life when compared to someone like Cook.

"Lord, be with Cook. Strengthen her heart and make her whole again." Memories of the anguish Richard had expressed in private drew her back to the moments in the garden just before she'd let him know she was there.

He loved Cook. She certainly had a personality that won folks over, but Richard's love surpassed that. It was as if his own mother were dying in the house. Cook had told Isabella that his parents died when he was a boy and he had no real memory of his own mother, only the memories his nanna, his name for his aunt Bea, had given him. Bea had become Richard's only real mother. What part did Cook play in his life? His grandmother. . .of course. Isabella should have realized that before. Cook had no problem telling the young man what he should or should not do, and yet she also would step back and let him make his own choices. Yes, she was his grandmother, a woman who unconditionally loved him and didn't have to be the one to always discipline him.

"Oh, Richard, no wonder your heart is breaking." Fresh tears burned the edges of her eyes. She buried her face in a pillow. "Lord, I would have loved to have held Richard in my arms and kissed him." But did he really want to kiss her—or was he seeking consolation because of his anguish over Cook?

"How can I show Richard that I care for him while I still honor my parents, Lord?"

A gentle knock on her door stopped her prayer. Isabella got up and opened it.

"Are you okay, Isabella?"

"I'm fine, Mima." She slipped back into her room, leaving the door open for her mother to follow.

"I wasn't aware that you've become so close to Francine Hunte."

"Francine?"

"Cook's real name." Her mother sat down on the bed beside her.

"Oh, sorry. She's a sweet woman."

"Sí, I've heard she has a tremendous heart for others and has never minced words. But that still doesn't explain how you could have such deep feelings, having known her for such a little time."

"I guess I'm more concerned for Richard."

"Richard? I see. Should we be talking about something else?"

"No, Mima, not really." She couldn't tell her parents. They wouldn't understand. They'd insist that Richard marry her for the sake of her virtue. Of course, he hadn't kissed her, so maybe they wouldn't go that far.

"Your feelings for Señor Southard are growing?"

"Sí." Isabella folded and unfolded her fingers.

"How often do you see him alone?"

"Very seldom. It's amazing that I can work in his home and work for him, and he's never around. He leaves me messages and I leave him some. I think we've been alone discussing the books maybe three times in the past couple of weeks."

"Then how is it you've come to have stronger feelings for him?"

"I don't know, Mima. I'm fighting them but. . ."

"But your heart has decided differently, yes?"

"Yes, Mima."

"And how does Richard feel about you?"

"I don't know, Mima. Please don't embarrass me and speak to him. I know it is our custom but. . ."

"But you wish not to have us approach him until you are certain about how he feels?"

"Sí, Mima, you understand?" Isabella breathed a sigh of relief.

"Sí, I understand. I think it's foolish, but if it is as you say, and you do not spend time alone with him, then we can wait for awhile."

"*Gracías,* Mima. His heart is breaking over Cook. I would hate for him to have to speak with you and Papá at this time."

Yolanda reached out and captured her hands. "Tell me the truth, Isabella, have you and Richard spoken about private matters?"

eight

Richard checked on Cook as she slept. He found Lizzy sitting in a rocker next to her mother's bed. "Lizzy, I made up a bed with fresh linens for you, if you're inclined to sleep."

"Thank you, but I'll probably stay right here for tonight."

"Wherever you're more comfortable. Can I get you a cup of tea or something?"

"No, thank you, I'm fine."

"All right, I'll see you in the morning. I'll be in my office for a bit, then I'm going to try and get some rest."

"Good night, Richard. Thank you."

"Anything for Cook." The words stuck in his throat.

He slipped out of the room and went to his office. Earlier he had penned a letter to his uncle and sent it to town with a courier in the hope it would sail out with the first ship heading north. Somehow, he'd need to focus on work. He sat at his desk and pulled out a sheet of paper to write a note for Isabella. He dipped his pen and poised it over the paper. What should he say? What did he need done? Honestly, he hadn't gone over her work today, not with Cook's emergency. Putting his pen down, he reached for the ledgers. There on top of them lay a single piece of paper and an opened envelope. "What's this?"

Richard opened the folded sheet of paper.

Dear Richard,
  I tried to bring this to your attention earlier, but I couldn't find you at the docks. Please let me know what you would like me to do about it.

Sincerely,
Isabella

Richard found himself tracing her signature with his finger. Why had he almost kissed her earlier today? Whatever possessed him to attempt such a thing?

My emotions regarding Cook must have gotten the best of me, he reasoned. But wasn't she about to kiss him before good common sense got through to her? Or had she simply been in shock that he would even make such an attempt? Would she even come to work tomorrow? With her father's strict code, she might not be allowed to go back to work.

Richard got up and began to pace. What should he do? Should he go to her home and explain? *Explain what?* He turned and paced in the opposite direction. *That I almost impulsively kissed her?* He groaned. Would he have to promise marriage in order for her to continue working for him?

No, he could hire others to do his bookwork. Now that he was beginning to have more time, he could do his own books. Didn't Micah mention the possibility of having her work for him a few hours a week? Perhaps there were other businessmen who might be interested in hiring her also. Now that she had the experience of working for him, she'd be more hirable.

Maybe it's for the best. I need to spend more time at home to help watch over Cook, and I can't do that with Isabella there. "Lord, heal Cook, please," he whispered, his hundredth prayer for the day.

A knock on the front door pulled him out of his meandering and brought him back to the present. "Who could it be at this hour?" he wondered aloud.

Lizzy leaned out of her mother's doorway. "Who is it?"

"Don't know. I'll get it. Stay with your mother." Richard approached the front entrance as the second knock rattled the door in its hinges.

A young man, perhaps fourteen, stood at his door with a folder under his arm.

"May I help you?"

"Package for Mr. Southard."

"That's me." Richard pulled a fifty-cent piece out of his pants pocket. "Thank you."

The young man jumped off the porch and ran back toward town. Richard closed the door with his foot and opened the sealed file. "What can this be?"

As he thumbed through the pages, he discovered it was Dabney's offer. The paperwork was very detailed and had obviously been drawn up by a lawyer. "I'll have to look at these carefully."

Richard tossed them on the left-hand corner of his desk, where he noticed the letter Isabella had mentioned in her note. He reached for it and pulled out the thin onionskin paper. He scanned the first words and collapsed on his chair.

❧

Isabella tossed and turned. She'd been so caught up with Cook and the aborted kiss, she'd forgotten about the letter Richard had received earlier today. Should she tell her parents? A letter was a private matter, but maybe they could help. Richard was a proud man and might be offended if her parents interfered. And if she said something, he might lose confidence in her ability to keep private matters confidential.

Unable to sleep, she dressed and decided to take a walk to the beach. The gentle lull of the waves as they rolled up on the shore calmed her haggard nerves. "What a day, Lord. I know I should be able to rest in You and Your peace but. . . I'm just not doing a good job."

Isabella sat down on the sand and let the fine bits of broken coral and shells flow through her hands. The full moon painted the night sky in rich blues. She took in a deep breath and released it slowly. There was something about the ocean that always calmed her.

"Father, I'm so confused."

"Isabella."

"Richard?" When she turned, she saw that his blond curls

were like spun gold in the moonlight. "What are you doing here?"

"I followed you. I was outside your home debating about knocking and waking up your family when I saw you slip out. What are you doing out here at this time of night?"

"I. . .I couldn't sleep."

Richard sat down beside her. "We have to talk."

"Sí."

"I'm attracted to you, Isabella, but I can't consider marriage, at least not now. I'm responsible for too many things. A romance, a marriage, would take away from my work."

"I was joking about the marriage."

Richard knitted his eyebrows.

"All right, yes, my father would have insisted you marry me if you kissed me."

A crooked grin lifted his lips.

"You know my family customs very well."

"I grew up here. I've known several Hispanic families. Most were from Cuba, but there are some from other countries."

"With the cigar industry there are many of us here now." She hesitated. "What are you going to do about Manuel's letter? He says he can wait no longer for you to send the money?"

Richard picked up a stone and tossed it into the waves. "I don't know. Just today a man offered to give me a loan to get the boat out of Havana. I might have to take him up on it, although the paperwork he sent me looks like a study in legal double-talk."

"I'm so sorry. At the time I thought it unfair of Manuel to offer such a thing to you. My father fought with him for a long time on the matter, but Manuel could not be moved."

"Thank you for telling me that."

"I'm glad you understand our ways."

"We have a few of our own, also. But growing up here, I've learned a lot about the various cultures that exist in the world. Back on the farmstead in upper New York State, we were all the same, our families going back many generations."

"In Cuba, it is that way, also."

Richard picked up a handful of sand and let it stream through his fingers. "What brought your family here from Cuba?"

"Work. Papá got a job rolling cigars. He felt there might be more opportunities for him here. But he does just the same as he did back in Cuba."

"Do you want to return to Cuba?"

"No, I like it here. I like the freedoms."

Richard placed his hand on hers. "Isabella, if someone sees us talking, your father would insist we get engaged."

"I know, but I also enjoy speaking with you."

"And I enjoy speaking with you." He kissed the top of her hand. "Shall I ask permission to escort you to dinner some evening?"

"No, Richard, then Papá would not allow me to work for you."

"Wouldn't you like to see if we could develop a relationship?"

"Yes, very much, but you don't understand. In order for me to not be paired off with someone, I had to get a job. My father is ready to have me married. It's not that I object to marriage—I would like to get married one day. It's just that I want to marry for love. Oh, I know I could eventually fall in love with the man Papá would choose, and he would choose wisely. But I guess I've lived in this country long enough to want what others have."

He released her hand. "I understand, and I will not ask your father. But I can't continue to dishonor your father by talking with you. Mr. Bower has asked me if you might be interested in doing some bookwork for him. And I believe there will be others. Perhaps if you start working for a variety of businesses, we might then be free to explore a relationship."

"Didn't you just say you didn't have time for a romance?" *Why is he trying to find other work for me? Am I not doing a good enough job?*

Richard grabbed another handful of sand. "Okay, so my willpower hasn't caught up to my brain yet. If we continue talking with each other, your parents will not be happy."

"True."

"What's the answer? Do I ask to court you so that we can talk?" Richard well understood the custom; if he asked to court Isabella, that would mean he was also interested in marriage.

"That won't work. We'd have to be chaperoned every minute we were together."

"All right, then we won't talk about anything except business. . .or what's left of my business."

"How are you going to get the money to get your boat back from Manuel? Will you take it from your savings? Manuel said he would take the other man's offer by the end of the month."

"I honestly don't know. I'll have to keep praying and seeking the Lord's wisdom because I'm fresh out."

"Would you like my father to talk with Manuel?"

"No, I don't think that will help. I can't blame Manuel, and since some of the islanders have made it clear that it will be a good sixty days before they have all the debts cleared, I understand his concerns."

"I don't understand," Isabella continued cautiously, "how you could go to Cuba on good faith and not only leave your ship there for the others but use up your own funds as well, and no one seems to notice."

"Some notice, but I guess I believe in what the Bible says about your right hand not knowing what your left hand is doing."

"Richard, you've put yourself and your uncle's business at risk extending help to others."

"I know, and the Bible also says not to be a lender. I'm not sure where I went wrong or how to balance the needs of everyone and my own."

"I'll pray for you." Isabella covered his hand with hers and gave it a gentle squeeze.

He captured her fingers with his own. "Isabella," he whispered.

She placed her other hand gently across his mouth. "Shh, don't say it."

Richard closed his eyes and nodded. "Let me walk you home." Richard got up and extended his hand.

"Gracías, but I better go on my own."

His fingers slipped through hers, leaving a burning path of desire. How could they obey her parents and still get to know one another?

And how can I fight my growing desires for him? She looked up at the stars and fired off yet another prayer for the Lord to help.

ↄa

Richard followed Isabella at a distance. While she didn't seem to need his protection, he'd be less of a man if he didn't watch over her. And who was he fooling anyway? He was attracted to her to the point of wanting to pursue a relationship, although a commitment of marriage at this point seemed completely out of the question. The idea of being married to Isabella wasn't a negative prospect, he had to admit, but he wasn't ready to take on the responsibilities of a wife. At least not until he settled what he was going to do with his life. Would Isabella even be interested in moving north if he should decide to stay on the farm? Or would she like the idea of going west and settling the untamed land? All things one would need to talk about long before they fell in love, he hoped.

Isabella slid through her open front door and waved.

Richard stifled a chuckle. She knew he had followed her home. He worked his way back through the streets to his own home.

A light burned dimly in Cook's room. "Hang on, Cook," he whispered as he walked by.

The next morning Richard brought the legal documents to a lawyer. As he suspected, the interest was high; and the slightest delay in payment would not only forfeit the boat to Marc Dabney, but the business could ultimately be lost to him as well. A loan from Marc Dabney on those conditions was totally out of the question. Even if he lost the boat to Manuel, he'd still own the business.

Richard washed the sponges in the vat. The dock was now rebuilt. The debris from his building had been taken away, but there would be no funds for reconstruction for awhile. At least not until the end of the summer, possibly longer.

Richard watched Mo bring in his skiff. "Good haul, Mo."

"Thank ye, Richard." Mo paddled the boat to the dock. "How'd your meeting with the lawyer go?"

"Fine. Unfortunately, I was reading the papers correctly."

"Sorry to hear that. What are you going to do?"

Mo lifted his sponges onto the dock.

"Not much I can do. If I take the loan, I could possibly lose the business and the boat. If I let Manuel sell the boat, then I only lose the *Sea Dove*."

"Doesn't sound like an easy answer."

"Nope, but there are some men who might not be able to pay back their debt in time. Even if everyone who owes me paid me the cash I paid out, instead of ordering my own materials, I'm still taking too large of a risk."

"I wish there was something I could do. I have some savings, but I don't think it will help you much."

"Thanks, Mo, but unless it's more than thirty-five thousand, it won't help. And even then it wouldn't give me the amount I need to rebuild." He did have other assets, but to cash them would quite possibly cause other problems. No, he'd have to take the lesser of the two evils; it was his only realistic option.

"I wish I had the answer, Richard." Mo secured the nets full of sponges to the pilings for drying. "If you don't mind, I'm going to go home and clean up, then relieve my wife."

"No, please go. I wish I could be there with Cook."

"You'll be there tonight. I still have trouble picturing Francine lying in her bed. I can't imagine you'll get much sleep with all of us coming in to take care of her."

"Sleep is the least of my worries."

"I'll see you back at your house later, then." Mo waved good-bye and walked down the dock.

With all his worries about the business, he hadn't been giving Cook much thought this morning. "I suppose that's because Lizzy is taking care of her, Lord."

When Richard finished cleaning up the dock from the day's labor, he headed for home. What he didn't expect to see was a house full of strangers, the kitchen full of food, and Isabella giving orders.

"Thank you, Mrs. Williams. Tell Pastor Williams we appreciate the prayers. I'll give your messages and the food to the family," Isabella said, receiving the pot of food.

"What's going on here?" Richard whispered, standing behind her and giving Mrs. Williams a polite smile.

"People have been coming all day, bringing notes of encouragement, flowers, food. . . . It's absolutely amazing."

George Hunte, Cook's son, leaned up against a wall. "How is she, George?" Richard asked.

"She's doing better. Some color is back, and she's able to talk some." George rubbed his large brown hand over his face.

"Do you think it's all right if I go in?" Richard asked.

"She's been asking for you all day. You best go in," George answered.

"Thanks." Richard stepped closer to Cook's room, took in a deep breath, and twisted the doorknob. "Cook?"

"Richie, come here." His heart beat wildly in his chest when he heard how she slurred her words together. She looked so pale, so ashen, so lifeless. *God, give me strength.*

He knelt down beside her. "I'm here, Cook."

"I love you, Son. Don't fret. I'm going to get out of this bed. The good Lord ain't done with me yet."

A shadow of a laugh buried itself in his throat. "I love you too, Cook. I'm glad you're feeling better.

nine

Isabella retreated to the office. Where were all these people coming from? It seemed like just about everyone on the island had stopped by to express their concern. Thankfully, Lizzy guarded her mother's need for rest as patiently and tactfully as anyone she'd ever seen. Isabella discovered she harbored an appreciation for the refined schoolteacher. Several of her students had gone on to college.

Isabella checked her figures one last time, then closed the ledgers for the day. Richard's cash balance for salaries was getting mighty low. Perhaps he was concerned about how to pay everyone their salaries and that was why he suggested she work for others. Truth be told, unless he had other work for her, she would be spending a lot of hours doing nothing.

Maybe Richard merely treated her like he did everyone else, kindly and generously, thinking of others before himself.

Lord, it's my emotions getting in the way. He's trying to do what's right and I'm resenting him because of my attraction to him. Isabella's hands shook. Was it time to admit to her mother that her feelings for Richard were getting difficult to control?

"Isabella." Richard stepped into the room and closed the door.

"Richard, the door," Isabella's voice cracked.

He turned and opened it halfway. "Better?"

"Yes, thank you."

"You're welcome. About last night. . ."

"Shh, you mustn't speak of it. Would you contact Señor Bower for me and see when I might be able to start work for him?"

"Will you still work for me?"

80

"Sí, but only one day a week. Perhaps Señor Bower's friends can hire me for other jobs."

"Isabella, you don't have to leave."

"Richard, have you looked at your cash flow lately?"

"Yes. I know it's low, but I should have some payments coming in soon."

"You'll need them. I've got your books up to date, and I think my coming in once a week will keep them in order."

"You're very good, Isabella. I will certainly recommend you to others."

She didn't want his recommendation; she wanted his love. "Thank you. I enjoy working with numbers."

"I do too, but I haven't had much time for it lately." Richard's smile sent a flutter down her spine.

"What are you going to do about Manuel?"

"I reckon he'll be owning a boat at the end of thirty days."

"I'm so sorry, Richard. What about the loan?"

"Unless we can renegotiate another contract, it isn't in my best interest to borrow the monies."

"Again, I am sorry. I somehow feel responsible because Manuel is my cousin."

Richard stepped closer and placed his hand upon hers. "This isn't your fault."

Isabella wove her fingers with his. She knew she shouldn't, but her love and compassion for this man grew moment by moment. His blue-gray eyes ignited with passion. He stepped closer, behind the desk, beside her.

"Richard," she whispered.

"My sweet Isabella, you—"

"Shh." She pressed her fingers to his lips. "Don't. Not now, not yet."

"How long?"

Her entire body trembled. She turned away. She couldn't resist him and look into his handsome face. "We must be patient; we must wait."

"I will ask your father's permission to court you."

"No, not yet. I. . .I. . ."

"All right, Isabella, I'll wait."

She turned back to him and saw his head bent down, his left hand clutched in a fist, the right clenching the edge of his desk.

"When will you come back to work for me?" he asked, not looking at her.

"How does Thursdays sound? I can do your payroll on Thursday and you can give the men their pay on Friday."

"That will be fine. I'll see you Thursday." He lifted his head and looked at her now. His eyes were dull and unfocused.

"Thank you, Richard. I'm sorry about everything."

"Buenas noches, Isabella."

"Buenos noches." She picked up her purse and headed out of the office.

The house bulged with people. Some folks she recognized, others she didn't. Everyone seemed to be talking together in small groups.

"It's a shame," said a thin woman, perhaps in her forties, who stood wagging her head from side to side. "Don't seem right. Cook's been there for so many of us. We ought to be able to do something."

"Ain't that the truth." A young black man shuffled his feet. "But we's can pray. Cook be glad to hear me sayin' that."

"That woman could pray a tortoise out of its shell. But you're right, we can pray for her."

The small group grasped each other's hands and went into prayer.

Lord, be with Cook; give her strength; make her comfortable. Isabella added her own silent prayer. She continued to work her way through the maze of people. As she opened the door, she turned around and found Richard standing on the stairs watching her. An awkward moment passed between them. She took in a deep breath and walked out of the house.

Richard fought the desire to run after Isabella. She seemed so vulnerable. How could he call himself a man of honor when he continually put her in compromising situations?

He turned and continued his flight up the stairs. His emotions were wreaking havoc with his peaceful existence. He was glad to see Cook determined to fight and live a bit longer, but she still seemed so frail to him. In all the years he'd known her, he only remembered a handful of times when she'd been sick.

He'd scheduled a meeting with Marc Dabney at his office this evening. What he wanted to do was call Marc a thief with his ridiculous offer, but what he needed to do was try to renegotiate the contract. If Marc wouldn't budge, then he'd walk away. He couldn't sacrifice the entire business for a loss of thirty-five-thousand-dollar.

Richard found a fresh set of clothes on his bed and clean towels in his room. Even with all the people in the house, it somehow seemed cleaner. Lizzy must have been cleaning all day, just trying to keep from worrying about her mother. Nanna was like that too, always cleaning when something was on her mind. Richard grinned, remembering the time Cook forced Nanna to stop cleaning one day. *"You're gonna wear a hole clear through that floor if you don't stop scrubbin' it."*

Nanna sat down in the puddle of water. "I just can't stop thinking about it."

Cook waddled over and sat down in a chair beside her. "Ain't nothin' you can do by frettin' about it. What's done is done. Now, trust the good Lord to make it right."

Richard sat on the edge of his bed. *What is done is done.* Possibly he shouldn't have turned his vessel over to Manuel, but it was done. The men on the island who owed Manuel money for the supplies should be more concerned about paying their debts in a timely manner, but what was done was done. Richard knew the risks when he'd used his boat as collateral. Now he just needed to make wise decisions, and signing Marc Dabney's contract as it was wasn't wise.

He buttoned his shirt and put on his bow tie. He ran a finger through his collar to remove some of the pressure from the foolish contraption. *Who invented these things anyway?* He looked at his image in the mirror. It did make him appear older, more businesslike, but who would wear these things willingly? A final brush of his hair and he stepped out of his room and reentered the sea of humanity filling his home. All these folks were here, not for gossip, but to show their love and appreciation for Cook. Richard's throat tightened. A tear stung the corner of his right eye.

Politely, he greeted several folks and made his way out of the house. He took in a deep breath and headed for Marc Dabney's office.

"Evening, Richard," Marc greeted him as he walked through the office door. "Did you look over my proposal?"

"Yes, Sir. And, as it is now, I can't accept it. However, if you're willing to make some changes, we might have something to discuss."

"Excellent. Set yourself down there and let's go over it, shall we?" Marc's smile seemed way too friendly. Richard fought the stiffness of his spine and sat down across from Marc's massive mahogany desk.

Marc's round belly pulled some of his shirt buttons tight when he sat down.

"So, what are the items you'd like to discuss?"

"The lien you'd put on the business if the payments weren't made in sixty days. In fact, the way you have it worded, it appears that with the slightest delay, you'd own Southard Sponges."

"Hmm, let me look. I had my attorney draw these up. Let's see how he worded it."

Richard watched Marc scan over the pages and stop at the appropriate spot. "This is pretty standard, Richard. If I lend you the money, I need to have something to guarantee that if you are unable to pay me back for some reason, I'll have ownership of something to sell and recoup my loss."

"I understand that. But look at the line that says you will own everything relating to the business. That's unacceptable. The business and its property I might be able to see, but our house and our land is above and beyond the value of the loan. Even the waterfront property is worth more than you've valued it at. And the value of the business is four times what you've put on the contract."

"Hmm, perhaps we can remove the house and the land, but the value of the business, I'm not sure. Seems to me, without the boat, the business isn't worth much."

"The boat is an asset to the business, but its value does not exceed the value of the business. I can transport the sponges on other vessels as I've been doing for the past couple weeks. Granted it's easier and a higher profit to ship the shipments myself but—"

Marc raised his hand. "I see. Let me think. I'd really like to help you out here."

"That's not my only concern about the contract, Mr. Dabney. The interest rate is extremely high, and the time to pay off the debt seems awfully short."

Marc drummed his fingers on the desk. "Let's see. . . . What if I give you ninety days?"

"Possibly." Richard eased back in the chair.

"I'd have to increase the interest."

Richard wanted to scream, but the better part of wisdom and self-control took over. He set himself for a long night of negotiations.

After a couple hours, he left Marc's office, none too certain they would work out an acceptable agreement between them. For everything Marc conceded, he would add another stipulation. Richard agreed to see the new contract after it was drawn up, but he wasn't hopeful.

He undid his bow tie and let the ends drape down his shirt. His stomach growled. He hadn't bothered to eat before he went to see Marc. Now he was happy his kitchen overflowed with baked goods.

"Evening, Richard. You were out late." Lizzy stood in the doorway of the kitchen.

"Yeah, had a business meeting. What's good here?"

Lizzy chuckled. "Set yourself down and I'll serve you."

"No, you've done quite enough. Sit down and tell me about your day." Richard smiled. "I'm an expert at raiding the kitchen—just ask your mother."

"I have no doubt about that. I couldn't keep Benjamin out of the kitchen for a spell. That boy sure could eat."

Richard grabbed some fried chicken, biscuits, and salad.

"Are you sure you have enough?" Lizzy seated herself in the old oak chair.

"No, I'll probably go back for some of that pie and possibly some guava pastries over there."

"Richie, Mo told me you had an offer from Marc Dabney."

"Yup. Ain't a good one, but he made me an offer."

Lizzy played with the edges of the tablecloth.

"Why do you ask?" Richard put down his chicken and wiped his fingers on a linen napkin.

"I don't know if I should be saying this, but I think you might want to know. Your uncle had an offer from Mr. Dabney years ago. He turned him down."

"Marc said something about that. Didn't appear to be any ill will on his part."

Lizzy bit her lower lip.

"Miss Lizzy, what aren't you telling me?"

ten

Richard mulled over the information Lizzy had shared with him last night. Marc Dabney's lack of respect for black people certainly said something about his character. A nagging suspicion that Marc Dabney had waited twenty years to get his hands on the sponge business began to form. Illogical or not, Richard couldn't shake his suspicion. Renewed pride for his uncle formed when he heard about Marc Dabney's rude behavior toward Lizzy and how Ellis ended the matter.

"Sin abounds in the world, but each of us must choose how we will live out our own lives." He could almost hear his uncle's words of exhortation, telling him not to be like others, to be himself, his own man, not swayed by other's perceptions. The advice had served him well in college when duties of the farm and studies kept him from raising Cain with the other students.

Richard rubbed the tension from his temples. He'd been doing too much thinking. He decided to check in on Cook as a change of pace.

"Good morning, Cook. How are you feeling today?" He sat down beside her bed in the small rocker Lizzy spent her time in.

"Better." Cook rolled over to her side and faced him, her hair pushed back under a scarf. "Now, what's been keeping you up late these past few nights?"

Richard smiled. "How'd you know? Never mind." Ever since he arrived on Key West, Cook had a way of knowing things most others didn't. She also watched over this house like a hawk protecting its young.

"Richie, it would take a fool not to notice. I may be stuck in this here bed for awhile, but I'm not deaf, at least not yet."

"You know I put the boat up as collateral in Havana."

Cook nodded her silver-crowned head.

"Apparently someone's offering to buy the boat, and the thirty days is nearly up. Several of the men on the island can't pay yet. Which doesn't surprise me, but I thought Manuel and I had an understanding that it could take a few months. In any case, he's of a mind to take up the offer, and Marc Dabney is offering a loan to allow me to get the boat back. But the loan is certain death to the business if I can't pay in time."

"Never trusted that man. Not from the first moment he stepped in this yard trying to court Bea."

"Nanna?"

"Yup. He decided she'd make him a good wife. What he had in mind for a wife was a maid, to put it nicely."

"Lizzy shared with me another incident."

Cook chuckled, then coughed.

Richard placed his hand on her shoulder. "Are you okay?"

"I'm fine. Can't laugh too well, yet. And, it's as you say, I was never more proud of your uncle than that day."

"I've pretty much ruled out Marc Dabney's offer, which means I'll lose the boat."

"I'm sorry to hear that, Richie. Seems to me those men who owe ought to help out somehow."

"I spent hours talking with them. Some wished they could help. Others just about said it was my own fault for putting the boat up, which is probably true; but shouldn't they at least be appreciating the fact that I put my business at risk to help theirs?"

"Would be nice, but we aren't always rewarded here on earth."

"True. Anyway, that's what has been on my mind."

"Oh, I thought perhaps it had something to do with a certain pretty young lady who's been working in your office every day."

Richard sent his gaze heavenward.

Cook grasped his hand. "Richie, I know their customs, and I know you aren't being disrespectful, but there's been a certain look in those blue-gray eyes of yours, something very similar to your uncle's eyes when he first met your nanna."

Richard groaned.

"Tell me it ain't so and I'll leave it be."

Richard gazed at the small oriental rug below his feet.

"Thought so. I might be getting close to leaving this here place, but I'm not losing my touch."

"Cook, I can't. I gave my word, and if I were to ask to court her, I'd lose her as an employee. Not that she'll be working much for me now, but still, Isabella says it's not the right time to ask."

"She'd know. Respect her wishes, Richard. Honor the Lord and He'll work it out."

"Yes, Ma'am."

Cook rolled onto her back. "Can I get you anything?" he asked.

"No. I'm just not as strong as I thought. Son, I love you as if you were my own, you know that."

Richard nodded. "I love you too."

Cook's smile tugged at his heart. He fought the thought of her leaving him.

She continued. "You're stuck like a conch in his shell. You may lose the boat, you might even lose the business, but God always takes care of His children. All we can do is walk with our heads high and know we are doing what is right. You do that and you'll be fine."

"Thanks, Cook. I won't refuse any prayers you think to send my way."

"Already sent, but I'll send some more. Now, leave me, Son. I need to rest ifin I'm gettin' out of this bed before I meet the good Lord."

Richard bent over Cook and kissed her on the forehead.

The delicate mahogany of her skin tone had returned. She might be tired, but she was better than she had been. "I'll check in on you later."

Cook blinked and closed her eyes again. Sleep was good, he reassured himself as he slipped out of the room. He closed the door to his office and knelt down on the floor. "Father, give me strength. Help Cook, and lead me down the right path with the business."

He paused and listened to the silence of the house, his eyes closed, and he focused on images of heaven with God seated upon His throne and the crystal stream flowing from underneath it. "Help me, Lord."

❧

Isabella didn't bother to knock any longer. With Cook sick and Richard always at the dock, there didn't seem to be a need. She opened the office door. "Richard? Oh. . .sorry." She closed the door. Wasn't he supposed to be at the docks, not bent over in prayer in the middle of the office? Not that praying was a bad thing—she just didn't expect to see him there. "Cook?"

Isabella rushed to Cook's room. Lizzy sat peacefully rocking beside her mother's bed. Cook appeared to be sleeping. "How is she?" Isabella whispered.

"Fine, she's been sitting up this morning. She's taking a nap now. How are you?"

"Fine." But was she? She'd spent the entire night awake, pacing back and forth. Was it right for her not to tell her mother of the growing awareness between herself and Richard? She had promised. Of course, she only promised to say something when the emotions became hard to handle. But was she handling them?

Feeling awkward, she stepped back into the hallway.

Richard stood in the doorway of his office, his arms crossed over his chest. His silky golden curls and blue-gray eyes made her shiver in appreciation. "Good morning," she stuttered.

"Buenos días. Como estás?"

"Bien. I'm sorry, Richard, I had no idea you were in there."

"Nonsense, nothing wrong with walking in on a man praying." Richard moved aside so she could enter the office. "I've decided not to take the loan from Marc Dabney."

"All right." She sat behind the desk and sorted through a stack of papers on which Mo had scribbled the men's hauls for the past week. "Does this mean you'll lose the ship?"

"Most likely, unless the Lord has a miracle I'm unaware of."

"I'm sorry. I don't understand Manuel."

"He's a businessman. He might be taking advantage of an unfortunate event, but he's not being totally unreasonable."

"He should never have asked you to use your boat. He's done enough business with people from Key West to know they will pay their bills eventually."

"True, but we don't know what kind of strains his business might have been under. He might not have had the financial backing to float the credit for as long as some obviously needed."

"I hadn't thought about that."

Richard smiled, and Isabella felt gooseflesh rise from her toes to the top of her head. She broke their gaze and looked back at the sheets of paper.

He stepped closer and placed his hand on hers. "My Bella. . ."

"Mr. Southard, come quick," she heard someone calling from the yard.

Richard bolted and left her quivering from his closeness. *How could I have fallen so quickly for this man?*

Isabella stepped up to the window and brushed the sheer curtains aside to glimpse the stranger. Richard's golden curls bobbed as he ran with the man back toward town. What could have happened? she wondered.

She sat back down behind the desk. A gentle knock on the door caused her to look up. "Yes, Lizzy?"

"What was that all about?"

"I don't know. Richard ran toward town with some man."

Lizzy grasped the doorway. "Mo," she whispered.

"Oh, I don't think it was about your husband. Don't you think Richard would have come in if it were about him?"

Lizzy sighed. "You're right." She sat down in one of the office chairs. "Ever since Mother collapsed, I've been overly concerned about everything."

"Seems only natural." Isabella put down the payroll papers. "I can't keep my mind on work. Care for a cup of tea?"

"Sounds wonderful. Let me tell Mother, and I'll join you in the kitchen."

"Great."

"Oh, and pick out some of those fancy pastries the folks have been bringing by. It's horrible for my waistline, but they are delicious." Lizzy winked.

Isabella wouldn't mind having another guava roll herself. She'd walk home a bit faster tonight and work it off. In the kitchen she set the kettle on the stove and prepared the table with some bone china teacups. Bea Southard's collection of fine china was more than she'd ever seen before. Each was hand painted and of the finest workmanship.

"Pretty, aren't they?" Lizzy commented as she took her seat at the table.

"Very. Where'd she get them all?"

"Several were wedding gifts, the rest are a collection she had started as a child. Her father would indulge her on her birthdays."

"Do you know Mrs. Southard well?"

"Yes. She's possibly my closest friend. We've been friends for twenty years. I wish she and Ellis hadn't moved back to New York, even if it is temporary."

"Why did they move back?"

"For James's education. Ellis had cared for the property until Richard became of age. Now that it's been in Richard's care, I wonder if it wasn't to check up on how the poor boy would handle the business. Of course, there were never prouder parents. Richard had increased the farm's profit considerably. I guess Richard has to decide if he wants to stay in Key West and work the family business or go back to New York and work the farmstead."

Richard in New York. . .oh dear. Isabella's knees weakened. She flopped into the other chair. "I didn't know he was planning on returning to New York."

"It won't be for awhile. Of course, Ellis and Bea should be returning early in the fall. Bea doesn't want to go back to those cold winters after living down here for so long. One winter is enough."

"Is this her first time back in New York?"

"Oh, mercy, no, Child. They've been back several times. My Daniel would watch over their business, and they would enjoy themselves for a long vacation."

The kettle whistled. Lizzy retrieved it and poured out the steaming water. Isabella stared, focusing on nothing. If she married Richard, would she have to move to New York? Away from her family? To a place so foreign it had snow? Isabella shook at the mere thought of weather that cold.

"Are you all right, Dear?"

"Fine, fine." Isabella sipped the piping hot brew. "I could never live in snow," she mumbled.

Lizzy sat up tall and set a piercing gaze at Isabella. "What?"

❧

Richard gasped for air as his tried to catch his wind. "What's wrong, Mo?" It didn't appear he was injured, something that had run through his mind as he ran to the dock.

"Ye better have a look at this, Richard." Mo leaned over the newly built dock and pulled up the lines that held the skiffs. Each of them was cut clean through.

"What?"

"Appears someone took off with all your skiffs last night."

"Did you call for the sheriff?"

"Yes, Sir, then ye."

"Thanks." Richard leaned against a piling and raked his unruly curls with his fingers, pushing the wayward strands off his face. "Why would anyone steal our skiffs? They aren't worth much, and you certainly can't go too far in them."

"Beats me. But some folks ain't thinkin' like they should since the fire. Most have come together and worked for each other, but there seems to be a small group of folks just set on bemoaning their woes."

"That's true enough." Richard had observed the same reactions in some of the islanders.

The sheriff soon arrived, and after taking a brief description of the stolen skiffs, he offered little hope. He figured whoever had stolen them would have sailed out of port with them in tow. He'd put the word out to the captains to be on the lookout, but he didn't expect much help from them.

Okay, Lord, I must be missing something here. First, I get word that the Sea Dove *will be sold in Havana unless I can offer to pay the debt in full. Now this? What else could go wrong? Should I merely give up and go back to New York? Is that what You want?* Richard pinched the bridge of his nose and tried to concentrate. He knew God wasn't a vengeful God, but events like the past couple weeks were trying his faith.

Mo went home; after all, there was no work. Without the skiffs, Mo couldn't bring in more sponges, and if he couldn't bring in more sponges, Richard didn't have any revenue; without revenue, the business would fail. Richard slowly made his way around the waterfront, looking for any boats he'd be able to possibly buy. Even one would help some.

"Ahoy, Pete, how was the fishing today?" Richard asked a local fisherman unloading his haul of lobsters.

"Not bad." Pete rubbed the stubble on his chin and squinted as he looked up at Richard on the dock. "Heard your boats were stolen last night. Is it true?"

"Afraid so."

"I have an old dingy at the house. Ain't much, has a leak I never got around to fixin', but you're welcome to borrow it if you think it will help."

"Thanks, I may just take you up on it." Richard looked down the docks. So many ships. . . Some moored out in the harbor, other's bound to the docks, and not another one had been stolen. If he didn't know better, he'd swear someone was out to ruin him.

"Ain't much, as I said, but it's something. Ellis helped me out a time or two. I'd be happy to tow the dingy out in the morning to save you some time. You might be able to get two runs in that way."

"That's a generous offer. I appreciate it. Thanks."

"Like I said, Ellis was kind to me on more than one occasion."

Richard shook Pete's tanned, leathery hand and continued his search.

As he walked closer toward the naval base, he saw Emile Fernandez marching toward him. His determined strides and the tight set to his jaw made Richard brace for a frontal assault. Had Emile heard about his moments with Isabella?

"Señor Richard, I need a word with you."

"Buenos días, Señor Fernandez, como está?"

"Bien. . . No, I'm not good. I'm angry. My blood is—how you say—boiling red?" The short man seemed taller.

"Just boiling."

"Sí, boiling."

"What is the matter?" As if he didn't know. He'd nearly kissed Isabella, he'd spoken with her privately on more than one occasion, and he'd touched her hand with a loving caress. Oh, yes, he knew exactly what was making Emile Fernandez's blood boil, and at this point Richard couldn't blame him.

"I have suffered great embarrassment, and all because of

one man who would bring shame to me and my family."

If only the ground would open and swallow him whole, Richard silently wished. "I'm sorry," was all he could manage to say.

eleven

"Mima, what do you mean, Papá ran out of the house looking for Señor Southard?"

"What have you done, *Niña*?"

"Nothing, I swear. We spoke privately, but no one saw us, I'm sure of it." Isabella's entire body started to shake. She'd seen her father this angry once before. She'd never known what happened that time. He and her mother never spoke about it again, at least not in front of her.

"When?"

"The other night. I couldn't sleep, so I took a walk. He found me at the beach."

Yolanda pulled Isabella down to sit beside her. "I asked you to tell me if you started to feel—"

"I know, Mima," Isabella broke in. "But I can control my feelings. They aren't at the place where I cannot."

"If your father has heard about you and Señor Southard, you do realize you will be engaged?"

"Sí." *Oh, Lord, please let it not be so. If Richard and I are meant to be together, please don't have it happen in this way. I would never know if he truly loved me or was just being an honorable man.*

"I'm not going to be working for Richard more than a single day a week. Señor Bower also has some bookwork that he'd like me to do."

"Have you failed Señor Richard?"

"No, Mima, but I can't talk to you about his personal finances."

"Oh, sí, I understand." Yolanda held her daughter's hand. "Do you love him?"

"I don't know. I'm attracted to him, but how can you love a man when you can't even talk to him to get to know him?"

"There are ways," Yolanda winked.

"Mima, what are you saying?"

"That even within our culture there are ways to learn about a man before one is courted by him."

"How? Please tell me. I don't want to bring dishonor to you and to Papá."

Yolanda chuckled. "I suppose I've been remiss from teaching you the ways of learning about men. But you've never seemed interested before. Richard is special, no?"

"Sí, Mima, very special." And her feelings for him were growing day by day.

"How do you know this?"

"I've watched him and how he relates to others, how he's conducted his business. He's a very fair man."

"Perhaps you don't need your mother's instructions at all." Yolanda grinned.

"Oh, Mima, please tell me. How can I get to know Señor Richard without bringing dishonor to the family?"

"If you haven't already, you mean."

Isabella's stomach prickled as if she'd swallowed a sea urchin whole.

"If your father is not already upset with Señor Richard, then you should continue to observe him, as you've been doing. How he relates to other people in good and bad situations shows how he will relate to a wife. This is not always the case, of course. There are men who put up a wonderful image in public, but in private would beat their wives or worse. But I don't believe Señor Richard would be this way."

"Oh no, Mima, he's very kind. He waits on Cook as if she were his grandmother. I walked in on him praying for Cook. There were tears in his eyes."

"Sí, this is what I mean by observing. How does he react to situations? You've been with him when Manuel insisted his boat be used as collateral; you saw how he responded. You know more than most about his personal finances. How does he handle his money?"

Isabella opened her mouth to tell her mother once again that she could not share such knowledge.

Yolanda raised her hand. "No, Dear, I was not asking you to tell me. Examine for yourself how he handles his money. Where he spends it reveals his heart."

Isabella thought of the generous loans he'd made to some of the men on Key West. Of how well he paid his workers. . .yes, he was a generous man. And seldom did he purchase items for himself. Almost all of his expenses were for the business or his home. "Sí, Mima, he has a good heart, a generous heart."

"*Bien*. Now, when you decide this man is the man you would like to court, you need to approach your papá and me. Your papá will decide if he is worthy of your affections."

"But Mima, we live in America now. Can't I decide for myself?"

"Haven't you already? By letting us know you are interested in Señor Richard, haven't you told us your heart?"

"Sí, but—"

"Hush, *Niña*. Trust your papá and me. We will pray. I have already begun."

"Oh, Mima, I don't know. I'm so confused. To have Richard near me. . .my bones soften like a jellyfish."

"Ah, then I suggest you decide quickly. Courtship takes time."

"But Señor Richard—he isn't ready for courtship. He's a busy man."

Yolanda raised her right eyebrow. Her rich black hair, pulled back, accented her hazelnut complexion. "You have spoken with Señor Richard about such matters?"

❧

"Señor Richard, what do you have to be sorry for? It is my cousin Manuel I am angry with. I have heard he wants to sell your ship, is it true?"

"He has a buyer, yes." Richard relaxed his stance. *I guess I won't be getting married today*, he silently thanked the Lord. Although the idea of having someone as warm and passionate as Isabella for a wife was not a discomforting thought.

"I will go to Cuba and I will speak with my cousin." Emile planted his hands firmly on his hips. The man was ready for war. Richard couldn't help but be pleased that Emile wanted to fight for him and not against him.

"No, it isn't necessary. Manuel won't sell the boat until the thirty days are up. He assured me in his letter he wouldn't be doing that."

"He should not hold you responsible for other men's debts. It is not fair."

"I signed the paper knowing the risk. Unfortunately, some of the men who owe the money do not have the cash to pay their bills in full within that thirty days." Not to mention the debts some owed him.

"Is it true that your fleet of sponge boats was stolen last night?"

"Yes."

Emile wagged his head. "I've never understood stealing."

"It isn't something I could imagine doing, either." Except for that time when he was six years old and stole a pocket full of penny candy from Old Man Bennett's store. Richard unconsciously rubbed his backside from the memory. Uncle Ellis made certain he would never steal again.

"I shall ask my friends and see if anyone has some boats to sell."

"I'm afraid I don't have the funds to purchase any additional skiffs at the moment. Perhaps after I get a shipment of sponges off to market, then I will be able to."

"Was your money in the bank that burned down?"

"No." Thank the Lord for that blessing. "But the cost of the building supplies has stretched my resources."

Emile rubbed the day's growth on his chin. "Perhaps some of my friends can loan you a boat."

"I won't be turning down an offer like that. If you find someone, have them come to my house and we will make arrangements."

"Sí, I can do that. It's the least I can do for the way my family has treated you."

Without waiting for a response from Richard, Emile marched back toward town with the same determined steps.

Richard blew out a relieved breath. *That was close.* He would have to be more careful with Isabella. His business was on the brink of failure; meanwhile, he was spending his free moments remembering the lily of the ruins, her long wavy black hair cascading down her shoulders and back.

Stop it, he chastised himself. He didn't have time for daydreaming.

"Richard," Mo called. The huge black man came toward him with giant strides. Mo was head and shoulders taller than most men, but he also had the most tender heart Richard had ever seen in a man.

"Mo, what brings you here?"

"I've been lookin' for you. I brought my boat to your dock; it's fully loaded with some sponges. I went out and brought in a haul. Benjamin came out with me and lent me a hand. I'm hopin' we have enough time to go out again."

"You went out and brought in a haul?" He didn't know why this should surprise him. Mo had always been a valuable employee.

"Just did what a man ought to, given the situation. If we get these sponges soakin', we might be able to have a good haul to go out with Bower's ship first part of next week."

"I hope so. We need the money."

"I figured you'd be hard pressed soon. Don't understand why those folks who owe you aren't borrowin' the money from the banks and payin' ye back. Don't make sense."

"I didn't ask them to."

"Ye shouldn't have to. A man should just do it." Mo nodded his head once for emphasis, and Richard knew that was the end of the matter.

"Let's get to the docks and unload your skiff."

"I'm sure Ben has it all done by now. But he and I need to be gettin' out there if we're going to take in another haul today."

Richard looked at the placement of the sun. They had about four hours until sunset. "Tell you what, if you go out again, promise me you'll be back before sunset whether your nets are full or not."

"That won't be a problem. Ben's wife, Edith, would be none to pleased if we weren't back before then."

Richard chuckled. There were advantages to being single. A man was his own man. He could do what he wanted, when he wanted it, and didn't have to fret over being home at a certain time or not.

"I'll have these rinsed and ready for drying by the time you get back."

Mo waved as he stepped down into the small sailing skiff. With the late afternoon breeze, Mo and Ben would be out to the harvesting area in a much shorter time. Richard rubbed the kinks out of the back of his neck. Perhaps he should consider changing the type of vessels he used to gather the sponges. The small steam engines they were making now could enhance a craft's ability to get the workers out to the gathering area each day.

"Enough dreaming," he muttered. "If you don't get to work, you aren't going to have the money to buy anything."

Several hours later, he pulled at the net heavily laden with damp sea sponges. Placing it on the center of the dock, he began to squeeze the seawater out in order to put them in the fresh water tanks.

"Lord, help me. I don't know what to do regarding the business. Should I sell it while there is something to sell?"

Isabella worked her fingers over the dress she'd been trying to sew all afternoon. Anything to try and keep herself busy and her mind not on her father's anger. "How could he have found out?" she murmured.

She nibbled her lower lip. Did she know enough about Richard to want to pursue a relationship with him? She'd skirted around her mother's question. But her mother was a wise woman; she knew Isabella had talked with Richard about such personal matters. The hurt she saw in her mother's eyes bothered her. At the time, speaking with Richard didn't feel wrong, but she now knew she had injured her parents. "Oh, Lord, if Papá finds out, we'll be married before nightfall."

She pushed the needle through the delicate lace she was attaching to the collar of her new dress. This would be a dress for church and social occasions; it was far too feminine for work. If she wore it to work, her mother would be convinced she was hunting for a husband.

But do I really want a husband now? She put the dress down and began to pace back and forth beside her bed. Richard's handsome face, his golden curls, and his blue-gray eyes came into focus in her mind. She sighed. To be married to Richard wouldn't be a chore. It would be a blessing, an honor.

But he's not ready for romance. He's too busy working for his family. And would he be moving back to New York once his family returned? *Is that why he doesn't want to get involved, because he knows he's not going to stay in the area?* Isabella twisted her hands.

"Isabella," her father called.

She stepped toward her bedroom door and opened it. "Si, Papá. I'm here." She braced herself, holding the knob. Her knees started to shake. "What do you need?"

"Come here, please," he called from the front room.

Isabella took in a deep breath and eased it out slowly. Her moment of truth had arrived. With great effort she forced herself to move forward, one foot at a time. She rounded the corner of the hallway to find only her father sitting on the sofa. He seemed calmer. And Richard was nowhere to be seen. Tentatively, she stepped into the front room.

"Si, Papá."

"Come, sit with me. I have something I need to discuss with you." He patted the cushion on the sofa next to him.

Lord, help me. Give me the right words to speak, she silently prayed and sat down beside her father.

He cupped her hand into his. "I have to ask you something." His rich, dark brown eyes scanned her own. "Sí, Papá?"

Yolanda came into the room, wiping her hands on her apron. "It concerns Señor Southard."

Isabella swallowed hard and looked to her mother for support. Yolanda put her hand to her chest and sat down on the rocker. "Emile," she whispered.

Her father's gaze shifted to her mother's, then back again to Isabella, and slowly back to his wife. "What are you not telling me, Yolanda?"

"Nothing." Yolanda looked to the floor.

"I'm worried for Señor Southard," Emile continued. "Manuel has told him he is selling the boat at the end of the month, that he has a buyer for it. Did you know this?"

"Sí, Papá, but I couldn't tell you about Señor Richard's business affairs."

"I understand that. . .Richard? You call Señor Southard, Richard?" His voice raised a fraction.

"Sí, Papá. He asked us to on his ship." She prayed that was answer enough for her father. Yolanda rocked back in her chair.

"Is Manuel selling Richard's boat what got you so upset earlier?" Isabella nervously asked.

"Sí, I cannot believe he would do such a thing." Emile turned back to Isabella. "This is what I wanted to speak with you about. Richard mentioned his finances were tight. How bad is it?"

"Oh, Papá, I don't believe I should say."

He held his hands up. "No, no, not the dollar amount, but is he in trouble?"

"I should not say. But I will say I will only be working for him one day a week now." There, she hadn't exposed Richard's finances but merely stated the truth of her current job status.

"I figured he was in trouble. He has not started to rebuild his warehouse. What of all the monies he brought to Cuba?"

"Oh, Papá, he's a generous man. Do not ask me such information." Isabella bit her lips. Her father shouldn't be putting her in this position.

He tapped her knee. "I only ask to see if I can lend a hand. I feel responsible for my cousin's actions. How he conducts his business affects the entire family. I will not share Señor Southard's financial situation with anyone. I did hear someone has offered him a loan to get his boat back."

"Offer? Huh! I would not call that an offer—more like a businessman's thievery." Isabella had read Marc Dabney's offer. There was much she didn't understand, but when she did the math, the interest was horrendous.

"I'm not surprised, if it is the man I have heard made the offer."

Yolanda leaned forward in the rocker. "What can we do?"

twelve

Richard stretched the kinks out of his back. Morning came all too early today. No word had surfaced about his fleet of sponge boats. The sheriff suspected they went out with another ship during the night. No one in Key West would be able to hide the boats.

He spent a few moments with Cook before heading off to work and found her in better spirits. Her color was returning and overall health improving.

At the dock he found Pete's old skiff turned over and a fresh patch on the hull drying in the sun. Richard smiled. Pete must have worked on it last night. *Amazing,* he mused.

"Morning, Richard." Mo waved.

"Morning, Mo." Following Mo up the dock was his son William. "Morning, Will."

"Good to see you, Richie. Been awhile." The two men shook hands. Will and Richard used to play together, having grown up close in age. But Will had married young and was the father of two boys. "So, Mo dragged you out to help him this morning, huh?"

Will's broad smile spread across his deep chocolate face. "You might say that. But I'd like to believe it was more the idea of helping a friend in a time of need."

Richard slapped Will on the back. "Thanks, Will, I really appreciate that."

"My pleasure."

"All this yappin' ain't gonna get our work done. We'll be in before noon with our first load, Richard. Have the vats ready."

"Yes, Sir." Richard smiled. In a way, he seemed more at home taking orders from Mo rather than giving them. He'd worked many summers for his uncle, and Mo had always been his boss. He'd never been quite able to look at Mo as an employee, but more as a partner. Times like this he was more certain of it. If the family didn't want to return to Key West, Richard was inclined to suggest that he just give the business to Mo. Except Mo was getting close to retirement age; perhaps he wouldn't want it.

He waved to Mo and Will as they went aboard Mo's boat.

"Richard?" a voice called from behind him. He turned to see Micah Bower heading toward him. "Heard about the robbery. What can I do to help?"

"Do you have a boat going north soon?"

"Yup, leaves tonight. Have some sponges?"

Richard pointed to the large mound of dry sponges on the beach above the high-water mark. "That pile there is ready."

"Great, I'll have my men come over with a wagon and load 'em up. Who should they be shipped to?"

Richard gave him the name and address of his distributor in New York City. "This will help. Thanks, Micah."

"Pleasure to lend a hand. Who do you suppose stole your boats? Never heard of anyone ever doing a thing like that before."

"If I didn't know better, I'd say someone was out to ruin me. But fact is, the fire had nothing to do with me or my business."

"No it didn't, but someone might be trying to take advantage." Micah leaned against a piling. His blond hair had now become sandy brown. There weren't many on Key West with blond hair, and because Micah had the same color hair as Richard's, he'd always felt a kindred spirit with the man. Now, as a man himself, it seemed pretty foolish; but as a child, looking so very different from most of the people he played with, it had meant a lot.

"Word on the street has gotten around about Marc Dabney making an offer to lend you the money. Personally, I wouldn't be surprised if the rumor came from Dabney himself. He always seemed to want to make more of himself, and I think he thought this was a good horn to blow."

"Perhaps. I don't know the man all that well. His proposal was no real offer."

"You alluded to that the other day. What's the deal he offered, if you don't mind me asking?"

"He basically was charging about twenty percent interest, and I think it was compounded. I didn't take the time to do the figures on that. Then he had clauses in there that if I was as much as a day late with any portion of the payment, he'd essentially own the business."

Micah crossed his arms over his chest and groaned. "You didn't take him up on it, right?"

"Of course not. I'd rather lose the business than have it stolen from me legally."

"You're a wise man for someone so young. Who taught you about contracts?"

"School. Of course, my nanna had a hand in making me wise about my money when I was no taller than a sea turtle. She used to talk about 'seed money.' I think she called it 'corn money' when I was really small. Anyway, she let me know if I spent it all, I'd have nothing to grow with the following year."

"Wise woman, your nanna. A bit unorthodox for her time, I'd say."

Richard chuckled. "I think that's why she loved it so much down here. Back home she'd have to conform to strict society. Here she didn't have to worry about social rules. Although more of that has come to town in recent days, I've seen."

"Afraid so. As a town matures, social etiquette does develop along with it. Can't believe this little island has the second largest city in the entire state of Florida. Been exciting watching it develop, though."

"Heard several families were pulling out because of the fire," Richard commented.

"Such a shame. But I guess it's the way things are. Are you going to survive?"

"Honestly, I don't know. If some of the men don't start paying me back soon, I'll be in real hot water. I didn't expect them to not pay me back right away."

"Risky business loaning a man money when he ain't asked for it."

"True, but I thought they would have understood and appreciated that I went out of the way to lend them a hand."

Micah readjusted his stance. "I think most feel they are in your debt and will pay you back."

"Oh, I'm not saying they won't pay me back, just that I wasn't expecting them to tell me it might take months before they could."

"Months?" Micah whistled. "No wonder you're concerned."

"I'll be lucky if I get the warehouse rebuilt by the end of the summer."

"What about your ship?"

"Nothing I can do there. I figure it's lost, and what the men owe Manuel they will owe me."

"Listen, I'll do whatever I can do to lend a hand. I've got some funds set aside. Would you like to borrow some to purchase some more skiffs?"

"Actually, I was thinking about waiting on them and buying a motorized vessel or a sailing vessel like Mo has."

"Going modern, huh?"

"If it will save me money and allow me to make a profit, you betcha."

"That attitude, Son, will keep you in business. I've got to run. I'll take care of that order of sponges for you. Do you have a letter that needs to go north?"

"No, I sent one the other day when Cook collapsed. Wish we had a telegraph down here."

"Would be nice. Have a good day, and don't work too hard." Micah winked and left him there with his sponges.

Should he write his folks and let them know about the boat, the skiffs, and the problem with the loans? It would certainly let them know he wasn't quite the businessman he'd hoped to be. *Vanity, all is vanity,* he reminded himself. Perhaps he should write a letter. Perhaps Uncle Ellis could save the business. Richard certainly was running out of ideas. And there was always the possibility of cashing in some of his trust funds. But if he understood banking, they were being used at the moment.

"Señor Richard," Emile Fernandez called out.

"And here comes my other problem," Richard mumbled to himself.

❧

Isabella felt like a five year old being dragged around by her father. She hadn't been allowed to say a word, and why he needed her to come with him this morning still eluded her.

Richard's shoulders squared after her father called out to him, Isabella noticed. His shirtsleeves were rolled up past his elbows and he stood beside a mound of smelly sponges.

"Buenos días, Señor Fernandez, Señorita, como están?" Richard smiled, but his stance reflected concern and caution. He glanced at Isabella for a fraction of a second.

"Bien. I've come with good news."

Isabella wasn't too sure how good her father's news was. He'd been bending every man's ear he knew this morning asking for favors. Richard was a proud man, or at least she thought him to be a proud man. She hoped he would not be offended by her father's zealous behavior.

"What news do you have?" Richard asked cautiously.

Isabella observed the tiny dimple in Richard's chin when he was concerned. Normally, it was barely noticeable. When he smiled it was very pronounced.

"I have spoken with some men. This evening after work they are going to go sponging for you. They will be using their own boats, or they will go with another who has a boat."

"What?"

"They wish to help you. They have heard of your troubles and want to help."

"But why?"

Isabella knew why, and Richard would not be happy with the strong-arm tactics her father had used. He had pleaded with the men's sense of justice, their sense of honor, and their sense of national pride—all because Manuel was Cuban and had treated Richard poorly.

"It is a matter of honor. I am here to work for you for the day and I will go with the men this evening."

"Señor Fernandez—"

"Emile," her father interrupted.

"Emile, I really appreciate your offer, but there is little to be done at the moment. I have these sponges to wash and soak, but that is about all."

"You need more vats?" Emile surmised.

"I lost most of them in the fire."

"I can help you build vats. You can work with your sponges and I can build vats."

Isabella closed her eyes and sighed. Once her father determined to do something, there was little that could prevent him from completing his task.

"Emile, you need to support your family. I can't pay you."

"You insult me, Señor. I do not ask for money. I merely wish to repay a debt my family has caused you."

Richard folded his arms across his chest. The dimple in his chin nearly disappeared. "Then I accept your offer. I did not mean to insult you."

"Sí, much better."

"Isabella, what can I do for you?" Richard asked. "Please don't tell me you are here to work also?"

"No, Papá asked me to accompany him."

"I see." His forehead knit with confusion. Isabella looked down at the dock.

Emile cleared his throat. "Isabella tells me she is to work only one day a week for you."

"She is very good at her job. I will only need her one day a week until I can rebuild the warehouse. Then I will have more need with inventory."

"I see. She says Señor Bower wishes to hire her."

"That's right." Unfolding his arms, he relaxed them against his sides.

"He is a good man, no?"

"He is a good man." The dimple in Richard's chin returned.

"Then I should speak with him before Isabella goes to work for him."

"Papá!" She hated being talked about as if she weren't there.

"Señor Fernandez." Richard cleared his throat.

"Emile. . ."

Richard held up a hand to stop her father's protest. "No, Sir, for this I need to speak with you with respect."

"Oh?"

Isabella looked into Richard's wonderful blue-gray eyes and knew what he was about to ask. Should she stop him? Did she really want to stop him? No, she would like to be courted by Richard.

"I would like to speak with you about your daughter, Isabella."

"Sí." Emile's voice strained.

Isabella shook her head, no, ever so slightly, and she saw Richard's eyes flicker. He swallowed.

"I wanted you to know just how gifted she is working with numbers. I have been extremely pleased with her work. This is why I mentioned her to Señor Bower. You should be very proud."

"Richard, I am very proud. Now, if she would get this foolish nonsense out of her head to work and find a handsome man like yourself to settle down with, that would make me very proud."

Isabella felt heat crawl up her neck.

"With someone as beautiful as Isabella, I'm sure the right man will come around any day now." Richard winked.

At least now she would have time to think about him and whether she truly wanted to marry him and move so far away. Coming with her father this morning had not seemed necessary, but who can refuse a father? What was he really after? Had he suspected more was going on between Richard and she than would be allowed by their culture? If so, why wasn't he demanding that Richard begin courting her?

Too many questions, and she felt like a flounder flopping on the ground trying desperately to gather some oxygen to live.

"Times a wastin'. I need to get back to work. If you'll excuse me." Richard reached down and grabbed some damp sponges and placed them in a vat.

"No problem, I will get to work on some vats."

Richard had some wood that could be used for that purpose, but not nearly what he needed to keep this business pulling in a profit. Thankfully, the other sponge fishermen had taken employment in town rebuilding some of the businesses. *With my money.* He bit back the aggravation he felt toward the men who owed him the most. He couldn't hold resentment toward them. It wouldn't be right.

Isabella caught his attention with the gentle swish of her skirts. Why hadn't she wanted him to ask her father's permission to court her? Emile was walking toward the shore. "Isabella?" he whispered.

"Shh," she whispered back and handed him a folded piece of paper from out of the pocket of her skirt.

He slipped his hand over the paper and traced the delicate skin of her palm. "My Bella, why?"

"Read," she whispered. "Señor Richard, which day do you wish me to work for you this coming week?"

Formalities, for her father's sake. "Thursday would be fine."

Isabella nodded and left him standing there. He planted his

feet firmly on the decking of the dock. She didn't want him to chase after her. She didn't want. . . *No, wait until you can read the letter.* Richard sighed and slipped it in his pants pocket. *If only Emile wasn't helping me today.*

Richard pushed the weight of his body down on the sponges in the vat, releasing the remaining seawater so they could soak up the fresh water. After placing the remaining sponges in the vats, he set out hanging the sponges to dry. He strung them on strings and hung them off the pilings. Strings of half a dozen sponges drastically changed the appearance of the pilings, turning them into furry, brown-tipped poles.

Richard turned around to see Emile unexpectedly walking off. *Just let the man be. He's probably got something on his mind,* he thought, reminding himself it wasn't his place to dictate the schedule of a volunteer.

"Mr. Southard," Mo's fourteen-year-old son, Joseph, came running up.

"Hi, Joe, what can I do for you?"

"Tell Dad Momma needs him at your house when he comes in."

"All right. Is something wrong?"

"Grandma's asked to see him."

"Cook!" Richard dropped the sponges in his hand and ran.

thirteen

"Not Grandma Cook, my other grandma," Joe yelled.

Richard stopped abruptly. Having only grown up with one set of grandparents and having seen them so very seldom, he often overlooked that most folks had two sets. Mo had found his mother a couple years after he and Lizzy had married. Ever since that time, she'd been living with them. Mo had built her her own single-room house in the backyard. It took many years for the former slave to get used to freedom, but slowly she settled into her own.

"Of course, I'll tell him. So, how come you aren't in school today?"

"No school today." Joe's wide grin reached his mahogany eyes, his father's eyes.

Richard scanned the harbor. "There's your dad now. Why don't you wait and tell him?"

The urge to go home and check on Cook still pulsed through his veins. . .and what was Mo's mother doing at his house? He hadn't brought a lunch—it would make sense to go home. Richard slipped his hands in his pockets as they waited for Mo and Will to pull up to the dock. He could wait no longer. He pulled it out and read:

Dear Richard,
  Please forgive my father. I'm not certain what he has in mind to do tomorrow morning; just know that his sense of family honor is at stake. My mother is going to your house tomorrow morning to help Cook. I'll be there after I run the errands with my father.

  Your Bella

Isabella was at his house? What was going on? "Leave the sponges, Mo, I'll take care of them after lunch."

The four men marched toward Richard's house.

"Joe, what's your grandma doing over at the Southards'?" Mo asked.

"I don't know. The house is full of women. I only came by to get something to eat, and they sent me to fetch you."

As they approached the house, Richard saw half his rugs hanging over the railing on the front porch. Others, he later discovered, were hanging in the back. Curtains were on the clothesline. The house was swarming with cleaning women.

Richard stopped dead in his tracks. Something about a woman cleaning meant more work. Did he dare go in?

"Oh boy," Mo mumbled.

Will spoke up. "Dad, I'll see ya back at the boat after lunch." He turned to leave.

"Chicken," Mo muttered.

"Got that right. My wife did her spring cleaning two weeks ago and I still haven't recovered."

"Face it like a man, Son."

"Nope, she called for you, not me. Adiós." Will chuckled and hustled out of the yard.

Richard had wanted to see Isabella; now he wasn't so sure. "Do you think I could sneak in and get some food without being noticed?" he asked.

"Not likely," Joe spoke up. "There's a mess of food in the kitchen, but also three or four ladies in there."

"Why didn't you warn me, Son?" Mo sighed.

"I told you there was a house full of women."

Richard rubbed the back of his neck. "Guess we best face it head on. They can't ask us to do too much. They know we need to get those sponges in."

"We can hope." Mo stepped forward first.

Isabella appeared on the front porch. "Richard, Señor Mo," she beamed.

"What's going on, Isabella?"

"Several ladies wanted to help Cook out and give the place a good spring cleaning. Everyone knows she won't be up for awhile. They just want to do something for her. She's always lent a hand to so many."

That was true enough, and ever since Cook got sick, people had been coming that he hadn't really seen in years, everyone wanting to do something for Cook. But knowing Cook, Lizzy probably had to tie her to the bed with all these ladies here. "How's Cook taking the invasion?" Richard slowly climbed the front steps.

"Okay. Lizzy has a way with her mother." Isabella winked.

"Where's my mother?" Mo asked. "She sent Joe here to fetch me."

"Last I knew, she was out back by the old kitchen."

Another Hispanic woman came out on the front porch. "Señor Southard."

"Buenos días, Señora, como está?"

"Bien." The regal-looking woman stood beside Isabella.

The similar set of her cheekbones and nose reminded him of Isabella's. "Your mother?" he asked her.

"Sí," the woman answered. "I am Isabella's mother. Are you speaking of matters of business?"

"I was inquiring about the invasion of the island womenfolk on my home."

"Me llamo Yolanda, Señor Richard." She extended her hand with a chuckle.

"A lovely name for a lovely woman." Richard bowed his head slightly in her direction.

"You are a silver-tongued devil, no?"

Richard paled. "No, no. I. . .I meant it as a compliment."

"You can speak with me in front of my mother," Isabella offered as her mother took a few steps backward, allowing them privacy to talk.

"Thank you." Richard nodded at Yolanda Fernandez. This

is why she came out on the porch, to protect her daughter's honor and to allow them to speak. "Does she. . ."

"Mima is aware that we have spoken."

"And?"

"We need to be careful to always have someone with us when we speak." Isabella looked down at her feet. She didn't agree with her family customs, but she wasn't going to outright defy them, either.

"This morning you would not allow me to—"

"Richard," Isabella interrupted him again, "are you planning on moving back to New York?"

So she knew about that. Was that why she didn't want him to ask permission to court her? Perhaps she was right; it would only complicate matters between them. He could be leaving as soon as three or four months from now. "I am uncertain of where I will make my home."

Isabella nodded. The gold flecks in her deep brown eyes sparkled. Did he want to leave this woman? They knew so little of each other, and yet, admittedly, they were both attracted to one another.

Yolanda picked up a broom and started to slap the rug to Richard's left. "My Bella," he whispered. "Is this what you wish, that we no longer speak with each other?"

"No, but if you move to New York, what point is there in pursuing a relationship?"

Attraction wasn't enough to build a relationship on. She was right: They shouldn't complicate their lives.

"Very well, I shall not ask your father's permission to court you. And I shall be your friend, nothing more."

Tears filled Isabella's eyes. Neither one of them wanted this, but it was best, wasn't it? Richard fought the knot developing in his stomach.

❧

Unwilling to deal with her own emotions, Isabella avoided her mother for days, certain she had heard her whispered conversation with Richard. Isabella had seen him working on his dock, but kept herself in the shadows. If she didn't want to develop a relationship with him, why had she signed her note "Your Bella"? she asked herself. And why was she bothering to check up on him every chance she could? It was like the days before the fire, when she hadn't yet spoken to him, admiring him from afar.

"Isabella," Micah Bower called to her.

Startled, she looked up from the desk and focused on Señor Bower. She'd been daydreaming again. "Yes?"

"Would you be so kind as to pull together the operating expenses for this time last year and throughout the remainder of the summer? Then go back and do a comparison of two years prior. I think I'm seeing a pattern and I'd like to check on it."

"Yes, Sir."

Isabella blew the ink dry on the ledger where she'd been working and safely closed it. Señor Bower had a larger business than Richard's, and its operating expenses were much higher. That probably had more to do with the products the Bowers imported and exported, she assumed. Sponges didn't take special crating or careful storage.

Over the next hour she worked on the figures for Micah. He'd been right; there was a definite pattern in the expenses during those months. She opened the daily ledgers for each of those months to try to discover where these extra expenses were coming from.

Her mind focused, she jumped when she heard Micah ask, "Find anything?"

She took a deep breath. "Yes, I was just starting to look at the daily ledger sheets to try and find the source of the increase."

"Don't bother. I think I know where to look. Tell me if the amount of the increase adds up because of payments made to Arcney Transport?"

Isabella slid her index finger up and down the pages, scratching the totals on a separate sheet of paper. If she subtracted the normal transport fee from non-summer months, she found the difference to be the exact amount of the increase. "Yes, that is the increase."

"I suspected as much." Micah locked his hands behind his back.

"Why do you use them in the summer months?"

"Because the rest of the year Ed Flanigan works here on the island. During the summers, he returns to Boston and spends the summers with his family."

"What are you going to do?" She closed the ledgers and put them back in their proper places.

"Not much I can do until I find another man willing and able to do the work." Micah stepped back toward the door. "Great job, Isabella, thank you."

She'd never heard of Arcney Transport before, hadn't even seen a sign in town for them. So why would they jeopardize steady income by overcharging every summer? Some business matters she didn't understand. However, she saw Micah was determined to stop the overcharging.

She reopened the daily ledger and continued with the figures she'd been given earlier. Her hands trembled after reading the name Southard Sponges upon a receipt. The captain had received five hundred dollars, and she was to deduct the expenses of the transport. Isabella thumbed through the pages.

Frustrated, she went through the pile once again—still nothing. She went through the completed file—still nothing. After searching for fifteen minutes, she decided she'd better speak with Micah Bower. She lightly tapped the closed door to his office.

"Come in."

❧

Richard thankfully deposited the five hundred dollars Micah had given him for his last shipment of sponges. He couldn't help but believe that Micah hadn't taken off for his own expenses, but at this point in time, he decided not to argue the point. If Micah wished to be generous, he would accept it.

He grinned at his bank account, which now boasted three thousand dollars. Some of the men had paid back smaller loans. He still prayed daily for a miracle. He had two days to raise the thirty-five thousand in order to have his boat released. The probability was slim that the money would come in, but he wouldn't rule out a miracle. God's grace was the only thing getting him by these days.

Cook was feeling better. For that, Richard felt especially grateful. She'd even begun to sit in the front parlor for small portions of the day. Lizzy had moved back home with Mo, which Mo appreciated. After nineteen years of marriage, he'd grown accustomed to his wife's home cooking. Lizzy still spent most of the day with her mother, but Cook was reaching her limit for constant companionship. Richard grinned and headed out of the bank and toward the rebuilding of the city.

Most of the debris had been carted away. Fancy new brick buildings in various stages of completion lined the streets. "Lord, if You see Your way fit to let me build a brick building for the new warehouse, I sure would appreciate it." Richard mumbled his prayer as he stood at the area where Southern Treasures had once stood. For years, Matt and Micah Bower had run their business from that dock, but when the area continued to expand, they purchased some waterfront property on the south side of the island, outside of the harbor.

Richard scanned to his left and saw the bits of remaining foundation of his warehouse and his new dock heavily laden with drying sponges. On the dock he saw a man and a woman. He stepped closer. Who would take a woman out on such a messy dock? he wondered. Having left hooks and knives all over, he decided he better get over there before the people hurt themselves.

As he got closer, a familiar profile came into focus. "Uncle Ellis, Nanna!" he called and ran toward them.

"Richard," they called back in unison.

Richard leaped to Bea Southard and lifted her off the ground. "It's so good to see you, Nanna. I've missed you."

Her gentle hazel eyes smiled. "I've missed you too, Son."

"Put your nanna down and give me a hug," Ellis grinned. "We came as soon as we got word about Cook."

"Have you seen her? She's doing much better." Richard was clasped against his uncle's barrel chest and slapped him on the back.

"Yes, we came in on the morning tide. You weren't about, and we headed straight to the house. You built a strong dock, Son. I'm proud of you."

Richard looked down at his feet. "After you see the books, I don't think you'll be all that proud." The books. . .Isabella had come in last Thursday. He'd left her a note. She'd done her job. She didn't leave him another note. He hadn't realized how much he'd been counting on seeing her for some kind of explanation.

"Nonsense, you did the best you could. I'm certain the good Lord will work it all out."

Richard's spirit brightened some, knowing his uncle wasn't disappointed in him. "But I've lost the *Sea Dove*."

"Cook told me. I would have done the same thing. Many of the men you lent money to have written me and praised your generosity to them at such a horrible time. They are also aware of what this has cost our business. They are good men; they'll pay us back."

"Not before the deadline in Havana, I'm afraid."

Ellis grabbed Richard in a playful headlock and rubbed his knuckles on the top of his head. He'd been doing that to him since Richard first came to live with his uncle. "If we lose the *Sea Dove*, we lose it. Not everything a man has to do is for profit. Sometimes our greatest tasks cost us more than others, and yet our profit is in the good will we've created. Besides, I might have some possible solutions to get the *Sea Dove* out of hock."

Nanna snuggled into Ellis. "Honey, let's take this boy home. His brothers and sisters ought to be settled into their rooms by now."

"James is still in New York continuing his studies, isn't he?"

"Yes, but it was hard on him to not come back and see Cook." Bea placed her hand in the crook of Richard's arm.

"I've been cleaning sponges all morning, Nanna. You wouldn't want to soil that pretty new dress."

"Nonsense, I've hugged your uncle when he was in far worse shape over the years. It's just a little saltwater."

"That stinks to high heaven from all the mud and small pieces of seaweed attached to the sponges."

"True, but I'm not going to allow a little smell to get in the way of being near my son whom I haven't spent any time with in months." Bea grinned and pushed them forward to their house.

"So, what's this about Marc Dabney offering you a loan?" Ellis asked.

fourteen

Another restless night of sleep plagued Isabella. The mere thought of going to work for Richard in the morning kept her tossing and turning. She didn't dare go to the beach to let the gentle roll of the waves soothe her, for fear she'd meet up with Richard once again.

Micah Bower had not charged Richard for the expenses of the shipment, and he'd asked her to keep that knowledge private. Richard had said Micah was a good and fair man; now she knew it for herself.

Isabella dressed for work in her most conservative outfit. She'd suffer from the heat, but it seemed wise to have a high-collar dress and long sleeves. She didn't need to tempt Richard any further, not that she'd been trying to. Maybe she *had* been trying to get the man's attention. But now that she had it, she'd been keeping him at bay. He had respected her request and hadn't come by. Today would be their second time working together since she'd asked him not to come around. Last week worked out perfectly. They hadn't seen each other, just passed notes concerning work to be done and work that had been done. Would he be in the office today? she wondered.

She greeted her mother as she left her room.

"Did you sleep well, *Niña?*"

"No, Mima." Isabella sat down at the breakfast table and ate the wonderful meal her mother had made.

"Ah, this is because you are working for Señor Southard today, sí?"

"Sí, Mima."

"Let your heart lead you, *Niña,* not your head." Yolanda

went to the sink and plunged her hands into the water.

"Would you want us to marry and move to New York?"

"No, but I will trust the Lord. I believe He dictates our steps. If they are the right ones for us to follow, He will help us."

"But it snows up there. I'd be very cold."

Yolanda laughed, then sobered. "Ah, but do you want to be cold at night by sleeping alone the rest of your life? Even here the single life is cold and lonely, unless the good Lord is calling you to be single. I cannot say, but—"

"No, Mima, don't say it."

"Sí, I will honor your wish. Just remember, your Señor Richard wanted to court you and you pushed him away, not the other way round."

"Sí, I know this, Mima." Isabella finished the last of her coffee and carried her dishes to the sink. *"Muchas gracías* for the breakfast, Mima."

"You're welcome, *Niña*. Have a good day at work."

In no time at all, she'd walked from her home to Richard's. The house seemed different. She couldn't place what was out of order.

The rich scent of bacon filled her nostrils. Richard must have cooked this morning, she thought. She went on to the office and opened the closed door. Papers and ledgers littered the desk. *What had the man been doing?* she wondered.

She dropped her purse on the chair by the door and immediately started going over the papers to put them in their right order, filed in the appropriate places. Her hands trembled seeing a list of income and expenses for Richard's land in New York. She placed it in the file and moved on to the next. "What are Bea's personal papers from her trust fund doing out?" she mumbled. This was quite odd. Richard would have no need to go over his aunt's papers. She tucked the paper in its designated file and again found private trust funds for each of his brothers and sisters scattered on the large desk.

Perhaps Cook would know what was going on, but she

didn't want to wake her. She'd been instructed by Lizzy that Cook needed her rest.

With the papers placed back in their appropriate places, she started working on the invoices and salaries for Southard Sponges. Richard had taken no salary, as usual. She went to the cash box to count out Mo's salary for the week. "Where'd all this come from?" she asked.

"And who are you?" a deep booming voice responded.

Startled, she jumped up and faced "Señor Ellis!"

"Now that we've established my name, I will ask again, who are you?"

"I'm sorry. Isabella Fernandez. Richard hired me to do the bookwork for him."

"Ah, he did mention that. Forgive my rude greeting." Ellis bowed slightly.

"When did you return?" She fumbled with the cash in her hands, glad that Richard had told her uncle about her, or else he would have thought her a thief.

"My family and I returned yesterday. You cleaned up the desk."

"I'm sorry, I—"

Ellis raised his hand to halt her words. "No apologies. It is my mistake to have left the place a shambles. We worked late into the night and simply retired for the evening. I thank you for taking care of it for me. Please, sit and relax."

"Thank you." Isabella sat back at the desk and placed the money on top of it. "Is Richard still here, or has he gone to the dock already this morning?"

"He set sail for Cuba."

"You raised the money to get the ship back?"

"No, I'm afraid the *Sea Dove* is lost. He's bringing some important papers for Manuel to sign that will at least transfer the debt the others owe him to us for the payment of the ship."

"I'm so sorry. My father is quite upset with his cousin for doing this to you."

"Tell your father it is the way of business. A good businessman can't fault another when he is doing what he needs to do to protect his business from ruin. So, how is it you love working with numbers?" Ellis sat down in a chair, placing his elbow on the arm and folding his hands together.

"I've always been good with numbers, ever since I can remember."

"Richard has always been good with them as well. How he managed to keep the business running while all these other things were happening surprises even me. Who is your father?" Ellis asked.

"Emile Fernandez. He works in one of the cigar factories."

"I believe I may have met your father, though I'm not certain." Ellis sat back, making Isabella more comfortable.

"Yes, my father says he has met you before."

Ellis nodded. "I won't keep you from your work. When you have finished with the books for the day, would you mind showing me what you've done?"

"Yes. Where will I find you? I don't think this will take me more than the morning. I'm supposed to work the entire day, but I don't see enough work to hold me here."

"Hmm, join us for lunch and you can show me the accounts afterward."

"Gracías, Señor."

Ellis got up to leave. She eased out a deep breath she'd been holding since Ellis walked into the room. Did Richard also tell him of his attraction to her? Is that why he wanted to socialize with her?

She wouldn't be seeing Richard today. Wasn't not seeing him what she wanted? So why was she sad? Isabella gnawed her lower lip and looked at Mo's ledger of the men's worksheets. Only one man had worked for a couple of days. Perhaps she didn't even have a morning's worth of work here.

She sighed deeply. "Lord, keep Richard safe."

No matter how encouraging Ellis had been, Richard still felt like a failure. Meeting with Manuel in Havana had been one of the hardest jobs he'd ever had to do. Hearing that the company who wanted to buy the ship had canceled their bid gave him some breathing room. As of this morning, when he left Havana Harbor to go back to Key West, the *Sea Dove* was officially on the market. They had a slim hope that the men of Key West would be able to pay their debts fast enough, and they might not lose the vessel. Admittedly, it was a very slim reprieve.

Manuel had been shocked by Richard's appearance with the title of ownership made out to him, and he agreeably gave the debt of the others to Richard. Once the debts were repaid, Ellis would buy another vessel. He'd reminded Richard that he ran the business quite successfully for many years without his own ship, and they could do that again.

Richard stood on deck as he watched the island come into view. Taking in a deep breath, he eased it out slowly, allowing the rhythm of the waves to calm his anxious heart. He wasn't perfect; he'd make more mistakes in his life, but he had wanted to do a far better job than this for his uncle.

Isabella's sweet face and ebony hair came into his mind's eye. He'd ruined his chances with her as well, although he wasn't exactly sure how he had messed up with Isabella. Perhaps their stolen moments alone—but if those had been revealed to Emile, he'd be a married man by now, or at the very least, engaged.

A wicked thought crossed his mind. If he let word get out that he and Isabella had talked privately, Emile was certain to demand an engagement. Then Isabella would have to spend time with him. But he didn't want to force a woman to be with him, and if he played that card, wouldn't that be exactly what he'd be doing?

"Lord, give me some direction here. I'm feeling rather disjointed."

"Mr. Southard!"

Richard turned to see Captain Daggett heading toward him. "Captain," Richard nodded.

"Does the end of your dock have deep water?"

Richard smiled. He'd hoped to persuade the captain to take a delivery of sponges up to New York. "Eight feet during low tide. How deep do you need?"

"That'd be pushing it a bit; she draws eight."

Richard scanned the pilings to see the placement of the tides. "It's about midtide now and going out. I can have the sponges loaded in thirty minutes tops, perhaps ten, if they are ready for transport."

"All right, point out your dock; I'll risk it."

"Thanks."

"I'll have a couple of my men go ashore and help you."

"I appreciate that as well."

"Join me at the helm. You can warn me of any problems on our approach."

Richard advised the captain as they passed his dock and turned the ship around for clear and easy sailing out of the harbor later.

"Amazing the damage that fire caused. I can see you were hit hard," Captain Daggett observed.

"Lost the warehouse and the dock. I hope to have the warehouse rebuilt by fall."

"Who's waving us on at the dock?"

"That's my uncle Ellis."

"Ellis Southard! I used to run sponges for him years ago. I should have recognized your last name. Sorry about that, Boy."

"Nothing to fret over. Of course, we're not the only spongers on the island now." Richard waved to Ellis. Look-ing down the dock, he was pleased to see bundles of sponges ready for shipment.

"True." The captain leaned down and shouted, "Ahoy, Ellis, been longer than a man paddling across a flat ocean. How've ya been?"

"Fine, fine. Been up north for awhile. Richard, here, has been minding the business. He's done a fair job of it too."

"You're still afloat after the fire. All things considered, that's better than some." Captain Daggett jumped onto the dock. "Richard says he has some sponges he'd like me to haul up north for him. Don't have time to chew the fat with the tide going out. I've got a couple men ready to help them for shipping."

"I'm way ahead of you. Everything on this end of the dock is all set. I hoped Richard might find a ship willing to take a load." Ellis winked.

Captain Daggett smiled. "Can see he learned well. Load 'em up, men."

In five minutes the sponges were loaded. "I'll stop by in the next few months when I'm heading north and see if you have any stock ready for shipping, Richard." The captain extended his hand.

Richard clasped his hand around the captain's. "Thanks. We'll be needing your help for awhile."

"Good day, Ellis, see ya next time." Captain Daggett leaped on his boat and hollered, "Cast off. Ready those sheets."

Ellis slapped Richard on the back. "Good job, Son. I'm proud of you."

"How'd you know to have a shipment ready?"

"Figured that's what I would have done." Ellis chuckled. "So, tell me, how'd things go in Havana?"

❧

"Isabella."

She turned. "Mariella, what brings you to town today?"

"Miguel was into everything at the house so I'm hoping a trip to town will wear the child out. What about you? I heard you've been working for my cousin. Are you enjoying it?" Little Rosetta sat down on the curb beside her mother. Isabella fought a smile. The young girl knew her mother.

"Sí, very much. Working with numbers has always been a pleasure for me."

"Thank the Lord I don't have to do any of the household finances. My husband does them. My interest lies in reading. Have you read the newest book by Mark Twain, *Huckleberry Finn?*"

"No, I don't think I've read anything by Mark Twain."

"Oh, you must. He writes so differently. The first book I read of his was *Tom Sawyer*. Came out in seventy-seven. I guess it kinda appealed to the tomboy in me. Anyway, it's great to see you again." Mariella tossed Miguel up on her hip. "Need to wear out the children before I have to get dinner ready."

"Adíos, my friend," Isabella smiled.

"Adíos," Mariella replied, and so did little Rosetta and Miguel.

They were so adorable with their dark hair and large brown eyes, Isabella mused. She wouldn't mind having a couple of children to raise. A fleeting image of a child with blond curls and her own peanut butter complexion flashed before her. Was it a boy? A girl? Only one man could father that child. Well, only one man she knew, she amended. She glanced back at the harbor. Had he returned from Cuba?

She headed toward the cigar factory. "Papá," she called, as he emerged from the building, his shoulders slumped over. "Papá, what's the matter?"

"The company is moving to Tampa."

"Why?" To move again. . . Hadn't they moved to Key West because of the company? Why did they have to move again? She'd never get a job in Tampa like the one she had now. If only she could find a way for her family to stay in Key West.

"I believe it is because of the union. In Tampa, there would be no union."

"So, you would be paid less?"

"Sí. Come, let's give the bad news to your madre."

"Papá, what about finding another job, one that would allow us to stay in Key West?"

"I know of no such job. I learned only one trade as a boy

growing up in Cuba. I could try and find work with other cigar factories in the area, but I do not think I would be the only man doing such a thing. I don't know of a single man who is happy to hear about the move."

"No, I don't suppose any man would want to work for less pay doing the same work."

"Sí, that is the problem. Come, your mother awaits."

Tradition or not, she knew only one man well enough to ask for help.

fifteen

Richard answered the knock on the door. "Evening, Micah, what can we do for you?"

"I'd like to have a word with you and Ellis, if you've got a few minutes." Micah ran his hand through his hair.

"Sure, come on in. Uncle Ellis is upstairs. Make yourself comfortable in the front parlor." Richard stepped back and opened the door farther.

"Thank you."

Richard climbed the stairs two at a time and knocked at his aunt and uncle's room. "Uncle Ellis, Micah Bower is here and he'd like to have a word with us."

"Tell him I'll be right down," Ellis called from behind the closed door.

Richard worked his way down the stairs a bit more slowly, then entered the front sitting room. Micah was admiring some of the collections his family had gathered over the years. "Can I get you something to wet your whistle?" Richard asked.

"No thanks. These are very delicate pieces of art. Where'd you get them?" Micah placed a small jade figurine back on the shelf.

"All over the place. Uncle Ellis started the collection before Nanna and I arrived. Since then everyone in the family has added to it from time to time."

"They're fascinating." Micah moved toward the high-backed sitting chair.

"Uncle Ellis said he'd be right down. Go ahead and make yourself comfortable."

"Thanks. How's Cook? Haven't heard a word about her in awhile."

"She's doing just fine, thank ya for askin'," Cook said with a wave as she walked by.

Micah and Richard chuckled.

"She's a bit slower on her feet—but I wouldn't want to test that theory," Richard teased.

"I heard that," Cook called back.

"Evening, Micah," Ellis said as he entered the room. "You picking on Cook again, Son?"

"Possibly."

Ellis leaned toward him and lowered his voice. "Good, I think it keeps her going."

"Speak up, Mr. Ellis, I didn't quite hear ya."

"Good." Ellis sat on the sofa with Micah. "So, what can we do for you this evening?"

"Have you ever used a company called Arcney Transport on the island?"

"Can't say that I have. Don't recall even hearing of the business. Why do you ask?" Ellis sat back in his chair.

"What did you say the name was?" Richard asked.

"Arcney. Have you heard of them?"

"Not sure. Manuel Fernandez, in Havana, mentioned an Arce Transport was interested in purchasing the ship, but decided at the last minute not to purchase."

"Arce and Arcney are pretty different sounding, Son," Ellis offered.

"You're probably right. Why do you ask about Arcney Transport, Micah?"

"I've been trying to track them down for a couple of days. I've gotten nowhere. Even the man who works for the company doesn't know where the business is centered. He says his pay is delivered to him at his home every Friday evening."

"That's a rather peculiar way of doing business," Ellis suggested.

"It gets worse. They charge me double what I pay the rest of the year to Ed Flanigan. Ed's been going back to Boston for the past few years, and he recommended Arcney Transport during the time he's gone. I figured it was an island company, they delivered on time, never had a problem with them. But I was doing some audits and I realized my summer expenses went up every year, then come fall they would return to where they were. By the way, Richard, thanks for recommending Isabella. I'd never have had the time to do these audits; I've been so swamped since Father retired."

Micah sat back. "I'm a fair man, and I wouldn't mind paying a little extra knowing I'm only using that company during the summer months, but double, well that's plain old ridiculous."

His uncle rubbed his hand over his face. "How do you get in touch with this company to let them know you have work?"

"I don't. Jesse Ryan just comes over the day after Ed Flanigan leaves for Boston. I always assumed Ed knew who to contact, never asked any questions. It's just some minor transportation needs from the warehouse to the wharf and some supplies for the warehouse. Ed's been doing the job for near twenty years now."

"Is there a postmark on the bill?" Richard inquired.

"Never looked. I'll do that when the bill comes in this month."

"You could send a post up to Ed Flanigan in Boston and ask him who Arcney is and how he heard about them," Richard added.

"I might just do that."

Ellis leaned back and draped an arm across the back of the sofa. "So how's the wife and kids, Micah?"

"Wonderful. . ." Micah went into an update on his family, and Richard's mind focused back on his conversation with Manuel. Wouldn't that be interesting if a Key West company was after the *Sea Dove*?

"Excuse me," Richard interrupted. "Uncle Ellis, what if someone in Key West is deliberately trying to ruin Southard Sponges?"

"What are you saying, Richard?" Ellis leaned forward and braced himself with his elbows on his knees. Micah did the same.

"Let me ramble for a bit. It might be nothing, but here's what I'm thinking. Someone had to know the ship was being held in Cuba."

"Just about everyone on the island," Micah interjected.

"True, but someone on the island also knew that I was managing to keep the business running without the *Sea Dove*."

"Go on," Ellis urged.

"Because after I had the offer from Marc Dabney. . ."

"Wait." Micah reached in his pocket for a pencil. "I need a piece of paper." Ellis reached in the small writing box and pulled out a single sheet of Aunt Bea's finest stationery. Micah scribbled down Marc Dabney's name. "Look at this." He scratched out the M from Marc and the Dab from Dabney.

"Can it be?" Ellis and Richard asked in unison.

"Hold on a second." Richard jumped up, left the room, and ran into the office. He thumbed through the files for Marc's offer. He pulled out the thick document and hurried back into the parlor. "I knew I'd seen or heard that name before, but I couldn't place it. Look here, on page eleven, three-quarters of the way down the page."

"He's still up to his old tricks, I see," Ellis sighed and handed the document to Micah.

"Okay, so we know Marc Dabney is the man behind the Arcney Transport, and we know he overcharges me, but I don't see how we can connect him to trying to ruin your business."

"I'm not saying Dabney's the one behind ruining the business, just that it's got to be someone local. Someone who didn't like me starting to pull the business together even without the *Sea Dove*, because that's when the fleet of skiffs was stolen."

Ellis sat back and brushed his beard. "And knowing that we can't come up with the funds to buy back the *Sea Dove*, he withdrew his offer to Manuel."

"Exactly."

"And I thought I had problems," Micah chimed in.

The front door rattled in its hinges. "Who could that be at this hour?" Ellis muttered.

"I'll get it," Richard offered. When he opened the door, he found a young man with a note.

"Richard Southard?" he asked. "Got a message for ya." He handed Richard a tightly folded square of paper with sealing wax on top.

"Thank you." He pulled out a coin, handed it to the young man, and closed the door. He wandered back into the parlor, wondering who could have sent him such an odd note.

"Who was it?" Ellis asked.

"I don't know. Someone delivering this strange note for me."

"Well, you going to open it, Boy?" Cook now stood in the hallway with her hands on her ample hips.

Richard slipped it into his pocket. "Later." He winked.

"Ain't good for my heart to be teasin' an old woman, you know," Cook replied.

The room erupted in laughter.

❧

Isabella paced back and forth at the edge of the shore. Why hadn't Richard come? Did he get her note? Or had he decided not to come? Hopefully her parents were none the wiser that she had slipped out of the house. Perhaps she should have gone directly to his house and not worried about the social consequences of her actions.

She sat on the fallen palm tree that formed a natural bench and removed her sandals. Unconsciously, she dug the sand with her toes. "Lord, please bring Richard here. I know he can help my father. I don't know why I've been so afraid of Richard courting me. I guess it's the rebel in me."

"Or that independent streak," a voice whispered from behind.

"Richard."

He gathered her in his arms. "You will let me ask your father's permission to court you now, won't you?"

"I'd be lying if I said I didn't want you to."

"Good. Is this what you wanted to see me about?" Richard released her and she sat back on the log.

"No. My father's company is moving to Tampa."

"Union?"

"Sí. They won't have to pay union wages up there."

"I've heard that's why most of the companies have been moving up there. So, what do you need my help with?"

"I don't want to move. I like my jobs. I know it's selfish but—"

He grasped her hand. "Is it only the jobs that you don't want to leave?" he whispered.

"No," she responded in the tiniest voice she could squeeze out.

"Good, because I can't stop thinking about you." He wrapped her in his protective arms once again. "I know your customs, and I know if your father should see us now, we'd be married by morning. But, honestly, I don't care. I wouldn't mind being caught if you'd become my wife." He grinned.

"How can you be so sure? You don't really know me. We've spent so little time together."

"My Bella, my sweet Bella, of course I know you. You're kind and considerate, a diligent worker, and you have a passion for life that goes beyond most. Besides, you've haunted my dreams day and night since you first spoke to me the day after the fire."

"And you've plagued mine," she confessed.

"I've prayed and asked the Lord if you're the woman He means for me to marry. I believe my feelings have continued to grow stronger with each passing day. Bella, tell me you feel the same."

"I feel it too. But what about New York? Will you be moving back there?"

Richard released her and clasped his hands in front of him. "That's something I still don't have an answer for. I enjoyed working the land, overseeing the property. Uncle Ellis says I get that from my father and his father before him. I feel it is in my bones and I can't shake it. I love Key West as well, but a man can't plant miles of corn and wheat here. He's fortunate to have a small garden plot in his backyard."

"True." She paused. "I've heard the snow is very, very cold."

"Ah, but, Bella, it blankets the land with a pure fresh covering. I often think it's like the covering we'll receive when we go to heaven. Light and airy, covering our sins."

"You did not mind the cold?"

"No, my Bella, you can always dress warmer. Here you can only take off so many layers of clothing to get cooler."

"My other concern is my parents. I wouldn't see them often. I've always wanted them to be close to their grandchildren."

"Hmm, there is no easy answer for that. I suppose we could try and make a yearly voyage back to the island."

"We are getting ahead of ourselves here, aren't we?" she asked and prayed he wouldn't say it was so, because at this very minute, she knew she wanted to be married to Richard, to bear his children and live wherever he lived.

"Perhaps I do need to ask your father's permission to court you. He might not find me suitable."

Isabella giggled. "My father is very proud of you. He cannot believe that you've treated Manuel with honor in spite of what he's done to you."

"The Bible gives very good direction on that. 'Do unto others. . . .' "

" 'As you'd have them do unto you.' "

"Exactly. I'm not a great man, Isabella. I'm a sinner; I have my moments when I'd like to strike out, but God wouldn't be honored by such behavior. If I were truly honorable, I would not be holding you as I have this evening. I know your customs, and I have not honored them. It doesn't matter if I agree or disagree with them. I should have more self-control."

"Set your mind at ease. I am the first to dishonor them by asking you to meet me here."

"I will do what I can to find a new job for your father. Does he have any skills besides rolling the cigars?"

"No. But he is a smart man and learns quickly. He's repaired broken chairs, tables and such, and refinished them. I think he has a talent. But he says he just does what any poor man would do in his situation."

"Okay, I'll keep that in mind."

"Thank you, Richard. I knew I could count on you."

"Let me escort you home before your parents find you have snuck out once again. Tell me, once we are married, you won't be sneaking out in the middle of the night, right?"

"No, I would have no need. The man I've come to see will be home with me."

"I long for that day, my Bella." He kissed the top of her head and led her home. They spoke not another word to each other and parted with the slightest squeeze of the hands. Her heart fluttered like a butterfly; everything would be all right. Richard would find a job for her father. They would begin courting. She silently slipped into her house.

"Isabella!" her father's voice boomed.

sixteen

Richard halted his steps upon hearing Isabella's father bellow once she stepped inside the house. Should he knock on the door? Or should he leave and let Isabella handle it? No, he should take the lead, and he returned to the house. "Father, help me, I need Your patience and grace, here." He raised his hand to the door and knocked.

"Buenas noches, Señor Fernandez." Richard purred the formal greeting, hoping to placate the man.

Emile Fernandez relaxed his stance. "Señor Richard, why are you at my door at such an hour?"

"May I come in?"

"Sí, come in." Isabella stood behind her father. Her cheeks shimmered with fresh tears.

"I've come for two reasons. One is a business matter; the other is a personal one."

"Sí, you are the reason my Isabella was out in the middle of the night, no?"

"Yes. She sent me a message to meet her. She's concerned about your move to Tampa and hoped I could help find a job for you in Key West."

"Isabella, is this true?" Emile asked.

"Sí, Papá. I didn't want you to be angry with me. I just wanted to help."

"You foolish *niña.* A woman should not be out alone in the middle of the night, no matter what the reason."

"Sí, Papá."

Her father turned back to Richard, his anger clearly appeased. "Can you help me find a job here on Key West?" Emile asked.

"I can do my best. Do you know how to swim?"

Emile chuckled. "No, I could not dive for sponges. That is young man's work."

"Isabella mentioned you are quite skilled at repairing furniture."

"I can repair some, but always out of necessity."

"This is not true, Papá. Show Richard your work." Isabella pointed to a rocker in the corner.

"May I?" Richard stepped toward it.

"Sí." Emile came up beside him and pointed out the various things he had done to the chair.

"Señor Fernandez, you should consider repairing furniture as a trade. You are quite good."

"A man such as yourself would accept such work?" Emile asked.

Richard knew that Emile wondered whether or not a well-to-do man would pay for such work. "Skilled craftsmanship is a fine art. As best I know, there isn't a man doing this on Key West, and you've probably found some of these furnishings being cast out by their former owners."

"Sí, I did not steal them." Emile's chest swelled with pride.

"I would not suggest such a thing. I merely say this to point out that many have need of the services you can provide. Perhaps you have a whole new business you could conduct here on Key West."

Emile sat down in the rocker and rocked back. "It would be satisfying work, no?"

"Very satisfying." A trade in furniture repair would take skill that Emile obviously had.

"I will give the matter prayer. Thank you for bringing it to my attention. Now, what is this second matter you wished to speak with me about?"

Yolanda Fernandez walked into the room. "As if you did not know, Emile. The boy's in love."

Emile looked at Isabella, then back to Richard. Richard

felt as if he had been put under a microscope. "Is what my wife says true?"

"Yes. I love Isabella and would like very much to start courting her."

Emile's face reddened and he looked to his daughter. "You have shamed me."

"No, Papá," Isabella cried.

"Señor, Isabella has not shamed you. She is an honorable woman and tries very hard to follow your customs."

"Then how do you know you love her?"

Richard sat down on the sofa, and Isabella joined him after her mother gave her a slight nudge in his direction. "Besides being the most beautiful woman I've ever laid eyes on, she has a heart that exceeds her beauty. She's thought often of her family before her own needs. A man looks for a woman who will love him and his children with such conviction."

Emile nodded.

"I have to confess, I wish not to merely court your daughter, but I want us to be engaged immediately. Señor Fernandez, my intentions are honorable. I want everyone to know Isabella is to be my wife. I knew some of your customs, but, I must confess, I don't know the process for an engagement."

Emile seemed too stunned to speak. Yolanda chimed in. "First you must begin by courtship. I would accompany you on every date as a chaperone. If I am unavailable, an aunt or grandmother would then accompany you and Isabella. You would be expected to buy the chaperone's dinners and any other expense of the evening."

Richard nodded.

"After a period of courtship, you would have to ask permission to marry Isabella from Emile. Then the time of the engagement is set by the father and Isabella's family. During this time you will also continue to be chaperoned. Isabella would begin working on her wedding dress and assembling necessities to set up a home. You, of course, would be locating or building your new home for your bride."

Richard coughed. "What if I already have the home?"

"This would be taken into consideration as to the length of time for your engagement. And, of course, we would host a large party to announce your engagement. That is, if Emile decides if you would make a good husband for Isabella."

"I understand."

"Papá, say something. You are scaring me." Isabella sighed.

Richard looked at Emile and wondered what was going on behind those dark eyes. "You should know that I might take my wife to New York, where I own a large farmstead."

Emile blinked and mumbled, "New York?"

&

Isabella trembled. She wanted Richard to wrap his arms around her again and make her feel safe but knew he wouldn't do something so forward in front of her parents. Would Father let them marry? Would he require a full year's engagement?

"Yes, New York. I have not decided what to do with my property there."

"What of your business here?" her father asked.

"Southard Sponges is my uncle's business and will one day be my cousin's. Since I have the property up north and trust funds my parents set up for me before they died, I felt I didn't need a share of the sponge business."

Isabella watched her father become speechless. He had no idea how wealthy Richard was. How could he understand Richard's funds were not fluid, but property and other assets that could be cashed in but would bring great financial loss if he did.

"But your ship?"

"Señor Fernandez, the hour is late. If you will forgive me, I shall return tomorrow and we can discuss my financial situation and how I can take care of your daughter. And I will try and clarify how I could not just loan myself or my uncle the thirty-five thousand Manuel needed."

"Sí, I would like to speak with Isabella privately." Emile rose from the rocker.

Richard turned to Isabella. "My Bella, forgive me for seeking your hand in marriage without proposing to you first." Richard took her hand and tenderly kissed the top of it.

She didn't want him to leave. She wanted to jump in his arms and stay there. But the time was not right, and she would wait and honor her parents. "Buenas noches, Richard."

He nodded and removed himself from the room, but not without having given her parents their proper salutation. She gnawed her lower lip and waited for her parents' chastisement.

"Emile, can this wait until morning?" Yolanda asked.

"No, I must know one thing. The rest can wait."

Isabella folded her hands in her lap.

"Do you love him?"

"Sí, Papá, very much."

Emile knitted his eyebrows and stepped back into the shadows of the hallway leading to his room. Isabella's heart beat rapidly in her chest. Yolanda whispered, "You should not have gone to Richard this evening. You've made this very difficult for your father. The only thing that has helped ease this situation is the fact that Richard has asked for your hand. Your father would have demanded that."

"Sí, I know, Mima. But I also know that Richard loves me, and even if Papá forced him to marry me right away, he would do it for love, not because he was forced."

"That is a good thing to know. But Isabella, you have shamed us."

"I know, Mima. I tried not to, but he was the only one who I felt I could ask."

"I understand. I don't agree with your actions, but I understand, and I will try and smooth things over with your father. Go to bed, *Niña,* and get some rest. Tomorrow will be a hard day for everyone."

"*Sí. Gracías, mi madre.*"

Yolanda slipped down the hallway and Isabella blew out the lamps. Tonight she was happy to know Richard loved her, that he wanted to marry her. This knowledge would help her face her parents in the morning. "Dear, Jesus, I have made a mess of everything. Please, help me make peace with my family."

Isabella removed her clothes and slipped into her nightdress. She lit the lamp beside her bed and pulled out her Bible. Sleep would be in short supply tonight. She would need a healthy dose of Scripture and time with the Lord before she faced her parents.

"Lord, thank You for having Richard come in. He helped Papá get control before he got really angry with me. Richard is such a kindhearted man. Please help me to be a good wife for him when that day should come. If that day should come," she amended.

It was still possible her father would move the family to Tampa. If he wanted to save face, he might just move them all up there with no one the wiser. "Oh, Lord, please don't let Papá move to Tampa."

❧

Richard walked through the dark streets to his home. How was he going to tell his uncle and aunt that he had gotten himself engaged without having spent any time in a courtship? Thankfully, it could wait until morning. By then he should have figured a way to tell them.

He crept into the house, removing his shoes before he entered, praying he didn't wake anyone.

A groan came from Cook's room. He dropped his shoes and ran to her bedside. "Cook, Cook, are you all right?"

"Richie! Good heavens, Child, what are you doing in here? What time is it?" Cook raised her head off the pillow.

"Are you all right?"

"I'm fine. What's the matter?"

"I swear I heard you groaning in pain. I came in to check on you."

"Ain't no pain I'm feeling now. Maybe I was dreaming."

Relief washed over him. She'd been doing so well, almost back to her old self again.

"Are you just getting in?"

"Afraid so." Richard stood to leave.

"What on earth kept you out so late? If you don't mind me askin'." Cook smiled.

If he told her what had happened tonight, he'd be up for another hour explaining himself. "Cook, I'm exhausted. I need to get up in a couple of hours. I promise to tell you after I return from work in the morning."

"Fair enough. If I didn't know better, I'd say you've hooked up with a woman."

Richard chuckled. "Good night, Cook."

"Night, Son. We'll talk in the morning." She pulled her covers up and rolled over.

Richard found his way to his room in the dark. The house was utterly still. In his room he undressed and slipped between the covers of his freshly made bed. A grin creased his face. It was nice having Nanna back home. His mind floated back to the images of him and Isabella on the beach earlier in the evening. There was a sense of peace or calmness that stirred within him when he embraced her, a sense of completeness. "Lord, be with her tonight; give her this same peace. I know that to her family this is a horrible shock, but please help the Fernandezes understand. And let me know if I should move back to New York or simply sell the land."

Richard completed his prayers for his various family members and let the lateness of the hour overtake him.

❧

At the sound of the rooster's first crow, Richard pulled down the covers and swung his legs over the edge of the bed, his eyes still closed. He braced the edge of the bed with both hands and waited a moment before rising. He needed to wake up. He needed. . . He sniffed the air, and the fresh scent of coffee infused his body. "Coffee," he moaned.

Dressing quickly, he found himself in front of a large mug of deep, rich Cuban coffee. The warmth of his first sip coursed through his veins, reviving his weary body. He took another.

"Up late?" Bea asked.

"Very," he answered, not pulling too far back from this life-giving nectar. He swallowed another gulp.

"Thought I heard you come in around two and figured you might need some coffee this morning." She poured herself a cup and sat beside him. She placed a loving hand on his forearm and asked, "What's the matter, Son?"

"Another cigar factory is closing down and moving to Tampa. Isabella asked me to meet her. She is hoping I'll be able to help her father find a job that would allow them to stay on Key West."

"Isabella Fernandez?"

"Yes." He put the cup down on the table. Now was as good a time as any to explain his actions last night. "Nanna, she's a special woman."

"Richard, do you know what you've done, meeting her in private?" Bea's eyes widened.

"Yes, I'm well aware of the strict Cuban custom. And I had been intending to ask her father's permission to court her, but she didn't want me to ask him."

"Why? That doesn't make sense, unless she doesn't care for you."

"No, she cares, but she heard that I might be moving back to New York. She had to decide for herself whether or not to even get involved with courting me, knowing she might have to leave her family."

"Ah, so has she changed her mind about that?"

"Yes, and I've asked her father's permission to court her, but they caught her sneaking back in the house last night. So, before he insisted, I asked permission to marry her."

"Oh my." Bea sat up straight in her chair. "Do you love her?"

"With all my heart. There's a lot we don't know about each other, but I'm certain the Lord is directing our paths. It's just a matter of whether or not Señor Fernandez will accept me as a possible suitor for his daughter."

"I think you forced his hand on that by meeting her in private." Bea fumbled with her napkin.

"True, but I could not allow her to face her father alone."

"I understand, Son. Will they insist on a long engagement or a short one?"

"I don't know. I'm willing to marry her right away, but I'm hoping she and I will have some time getting to know one another first. I think her mother will help smooth things over. She was very helpful in explaining what they would expect from me. Did you know courting a woman involved paying for the chaperone, or chaperones, to come to dinner with you as well?"

Bea chuckled. "I'd heard that. I've seen a time or two where a young couple would be at one table and three older women at another."

"Three?" Richard groaned. "I think I might go to the bank today and remove some money from one of my trusts."

Bea continued to laugh. "And what about the engagement ring?"

"Engagement ring?" Ellis asked as he entered through the back door.

"Your son got himself engaged last night."

&

Isabella stayed in bed longer than normal. She didn't want to face her parents yet. They were not pleased with her behavior last night, and while it was noble to try and find her father some work, it didn't excuse the fact that she and Richard had met alone and talked about courting and marriage. Isabella had shamed them. They knew it and she knew it; even if no one else on the island was aware, they were.

Hearing her father leave for the factory, she got out of bed and readied herself for work.

Her mother waited for her in the kitchen. "Your father is very aware of why you stayed in bed so long this morning."

Isabella hung her head, looking at her feet. "I'm sorry, Mima. I did not mean to shame you."

"Sit, Isabella. We need to speak."

"Sí." She sat beside her mother at the table, and her mother poured her a cup of tea and handed her a guava-filled pastry.

"Your father is going to speak with Richard and Ellis Southard today, if he can locate them after work. He agrees you and Richard should be engaged and that some time should pass before you marry. But, with the transfer to Tampa, your engagement period would be hard. He is scheduled to leave for Tampa by the end of the month."

"No, Mima, please don't go. Won't Papá at least look for work in Key West?"

"He will look, but you've put your father in a tough position. He is a proud man, Isabella. You should have known he wouldn't take well to the knowledge that you spoke to someone outside of the family about his employment."

"Sí, but. . ."

"No 'buts,' Isabella. You were wrong. You should have come to me and I would have suggested your father speak with Señor Richard about possible employment. He's not ashamed to look for work, just that you spoke on his behalf, as if he were unable to."

"I know; I'm sorry. I was more concerned about myself and not you or Papá."

"This is true. Now tell me, what private matters did you and Richard speak about last night. Did you kiss him?"

"No, Mima. I wanted to kiss him, but we did not." Should she confess the kiss upon her head? "Richard held me in his arms—it was wonderful. I felt so at peace from his embrace, Mima. Does that make sense?"

"Sí, it makes sense."

"He did kiss the top of my head ever so gently, at least I think it was a kiss."

Yolanda grinned. "Then it was a kiss. Papá will arrange a schedule with Richard for you to go out with him. He is free to come to the house and visit as long as either one of us is home. If you go to his house, one of us must accompany you. You understand, if you sneak out again to meet Señor Richard, your father will be very angry with you."

"Sí, Mima, I understand. I will not sneak out."

"Bien. Now, we need to start work on a wedding dress. I have no sewing machine, so we will need to stitch it by hand. I also don't have your grandmothers here to help me. We will need to work hard."

"How soon is Papá planning the wedding?"

"I don't know, *Niña.* It all depends on when Richard will have a house ready for you and how long an engagement he feels is necessary for you and Richard to get to know one another before marriage."

Isabella sipped her tea. How long would Papá insist on? And if he moved to Tampa in less than a month, that would mean she and Richard would have to court long distance. They might not even see each other before the wedding. One good thing about that, if there could be a good thing about the long separation—letters would be private. "Mima, could you and I stay on Key West if Papá goes to Tampa?"

"No, I will go with my husband. And you cannot stay here alone. We have no relatives for you to live with here."

Isabella's heart quivered. *Lord, please find Papá a job here on Key West. I know I'm being selfish, but I don't want to leave Richard. Please find a way, Lord.*

seventeen

Richard changed from his work shirt to a dress shirt and headed toward the center of town. All things considered, his uncle and aunt had taken the news fairly well. He knew he wouldn't need to tell Cook. If she hadn't heard him explaining to them, she would hear it before he returned home.

He stopped briefly at the bank and gave a note to the manager, saying he would return in an hour to pick up the requested information. Nathaniel Farris's jewelry shop hadn't survived the fire. However, many of the items had been locked in the safe the night before the fire hit. He'd heard Nathaniel was working out of his home until the shop could be rebuilt.

Richard knocked on Nathaniel Farris's door, and a gangly ten-year-old girl with red hair and freckles answered it. "Is your daddy home?" Richard asked.

"He's working," she answered and started to close the door.

"Would you tell him Richard Southard would like to speak with him."

She shrugged her shoulders and yelled, "Daddy, a man wants to see you."

Richard held back a chuckle. He'd done the same thing on more than one occasion when he was that age.

"Richard, what can I do for you?" Nathaniel asked.

"I need an engagement ring." He grinned.

"Come on in. Who's the lucky gal?" Nathaniel stepped aside, opening the door farther.

"Isabella Fernandez." Richard entered the roomy two-story house and followed Nathaniel to a front study converted into a small jeweler's shop.

"I don't have much, but let's see what you like first."

"I know nothing of women's jewelry. Nanna wore a few pieces, but by and large I haven't been around a lot of feminine jewelry. What is appropriate?"

"A solitary diamond is a traditional gift. But I've seen pearls, emeralds. . .anything that seemed special to the couple."

"Her family is very traditional." A smile curled his lips at the thought of how untraditional Isabella was. "However, she's more unique."

"Hmm, do you like diamonds?"

"They sparkle pretty enough; but I'm not the one who should like it, she should." Richard released a nervous chuckle.

"Ah, but a ring should reflect the beauty you see in her. Here, let's look at some stones, then I'll show you some settings."

Nathaniel gave Richard an abbreviated course in gemology. He soon knew more about clarity and carets than he ever wanted to know. In the end, he picked out a three-quarter caret white diamond with two small amber stones. Nathaniel said he could have the ring finished by the evening and delivered to his home. They guessed on the ring size, and Nathaniel agreed to change the size to fit if they'd gotten it wrong. Thankfully, Nathaniel's wife Julie's fingers were long and slender like Isabella's.

The engagement ring and matching wedding band out of the way, he went back to the bank.

"Welcome, Mr. Southard," Nick Farley said as he entered the bank. The short balding man sat behind his desk. "I have the figures ready that you asked for."

"Thank you."

"This is such an odd request from you. You've always known exactly where your accounts stood."

"True, and I still do." Richard examined the financial statement. "But I needed a statement from the bank for a certain matter."

"Ah, yes, I've heard of that mess in Havana. I had hoped

you wouldn't have to pull out such a large sum. The penalty payment will be so high."

"True, and I'm not withdrawing any money to secure the ship."

Farley's eyebrows raised.

"I also know if I pulled out such a large amount of capital, the bank could be put in a tough situation. I'm assuming these funds were used to secure the loans to the islanders?"

"Yes. You understand the banking business well. Many don't. They think we keep everyone's money in the safe at all times."

"I was taught that great wealth came with a great responsibility to others. My funds here are only some of my funds, as you well know. I would never compromise the security of your other loans. The truth of the matter is, while the *Sea Dove* is a fine ship, she's not the only ship; and once the funds are returned, we can purchase another vessel. And the value of one man's business does not exceed the needs of the community. At least not this family's business."

"Thank you. Now, what else can I help you with?"

"I do need to withdraw some money from this fund." Richard pointed to a small fund he had with the least penalties on it. "I would like you to put five thousand dollars into my personal savings account."

"Very well, you do understand—"

"About the penalties, I know. Do what you must." This fund was the balance of all his earnings over the years working for his uncle. He'd saved most of the money and used some for schooling. It was perhaps the money he was most proud of because he'd earned it himself. *What better fund to use to purchase your fiancée's engagement ring?* he mused.

On his way out of the bank, he ran into Marc Dabney. "Hi, Richard, how are you today?"

"Fine, Mr. Dabney, and you?"

"Fine, fine. Life couldn't be better."

Richard resisted the urge to question the man about Arcney Transport.

"You're just the man I was looking to find. I heard about your skiffs being lost. And a friend of mine has some used skiffs. He's pulling out of the sponging business. I was wondering if you might be interested in purchasing them?"

"Be glad to look at them. Where are they located?"

"Key Visca. I'm about to meet up with him. He's here in Key West for the day."

"Sure, what's he asking for the skiffs?"

"Says he's willing to let them go for a couple hundred."

"A piece?" Richard halted.

"No, no, for the whole lot of them."

"Lead the way." Richard followed as Marc Dabney waddled down the street toward one of the taverns. "What's the name of your friend's sponging business? Perhaps I know it?"

"Arcney Sponges."

∾

Isabella couldn't keep her mind on her work, and she left the Bowers' office early, her mind flooded with bridal gowns, white satin, and lace. Adding and subtracting numbers were buried somewhere in the midst of all that lace, but where she couldn't figure out. The additional worries of not having spoken with her father this morning only added to her concerns. She should have faced him. Then she would have known how he was feeling, if he still loved her in spite of her having shamed them.

"Mima, I'm home," she called and dropped her purse on a table in the hallway.

"Isabella, come in the sitting room. We have guests."

Isabella walked in to see Bea Southard, Peg Bower, and Lizzy Greene. "Hello." She found a seat and sat down, looking to her mother for an answer.

"These ladies are here to help us with the wedding dress and anything else we have need of."

Isabella looked at Bea Southard and flushed. "How, how, soon is the wedding?"

"We still don't know, *Niña.*" Yolanda reached over and placed her hand on Isabella's.

"Isabella, we know your family is alone on Key West. Each of us has a good hand for stitching, although no one compares with Peg here." Bea winked at Peg. "We're only offering to help. Richard is special to each of us, and since you are special to him, you are also special to us. However, we do not want to impose on any plans you and your mother are making. We are the laborers; you and your mother are the designers."

"Mima?"

"Sí, Isabella, this is good. We spoke this morning about how long it would take us."

"Sí." She turned to the women. "Thank you, it's a very kind offer."

Lizzy spoke up. "We're here to help in any way we can. The wedding dress is one thing, but if you need help with anything else, don't hesitate to ask."

Peg Bower, brushing back strands of her light brown hair, added, "I also would like to make something special for your wedding gift. What do you have in the way of linens in your wedding trunk?"

"Mima?" She looked to her mother. She hadn't put anything in the trunk. Her mother might have been putting in things, but she hadn't been planning on marriage, hadn't even been thinking about it until she met Richard. And since then there hadn't been any time.

Yolanda stood up. "Follow me." All three of the ladies followed her mother down the hall. Isabella sat stunned. Her future mother-in-law, or aunt-in-law. . . *How does that work in our situation?* A warm thought fluttered through her mind. *Our.* She was thinking in terms of Richard and herself together.

Isabella got up and followed the ladies' murmurs. She was surprised by the contents of her trunk. When had her mother gathered those items? After the women left, she sat with her mother and asked, "Mima, when did you have the time or money to gather all those things?"

"*Niña,* I've been collecting since you were first born."

"I never knew."

"Sí, it is something I wanted to do. Your papá allowed me to save and collect."

Isabella looked over the matching silver service for eight. She picked up a spoon and looked at the design. A small rose had been stamped on the handle. "They are beautiful, Mima. *Muchas gracías.*"

"You're welcome, *Niña.*" Yolanda placed the items back in the trunk.

"I want to tell Richard about these and the women coming to help, everything."

"All in good time, *Niña,* all in good time."

"Sí, Mima. I will wait."

"*Bien.* Now, why did you come home early from work?"

❧

Meeting Marc Dabney hadn't been providence. Richard suspected the man had been waiting for him, as if he'd been aware of all his actions. The mention of his visit to Nathaniel Farris's house triggered additional caution.

"Yes, I was looking to purchase some jewelry." Richard sipped his now cool coffee.

"Perhaps you truly did not need my offer." Marc wiped his mouth with his napkin. "I don't understand where Raphael could be."

"You'll have to tell him that I couldn't wait any longer. I have other family matters I need to take care of."

Marc grabbed his wrist. "Give him another minute."

Richard looked down at his wrist, and Marc released his hold. "All right, just another minute, but then I must go. Are you making a profit on the sale?" Richard couldn't help but ask. The fact was, he knew Marc Dabney had to be the owner of Arcney Sponges, just as he was the owner of Arcney Transport.

"A small finder's fee for locating a buyer. Only a trifle."

Richard scanned the dimly lit room. Seeing no one new enter, he rose. "I'm sorry, Mr. Dabney, I really must go. Tell your friend to bring the skiffs by my wharf in the morning and I'll give them a look over. If they're in fair condition I'll buy 'em. If not, you know the answer to that."

"Very well. Saw you coming out of the bank. Did you secure a loan to get your ship back?"

"Nope, brought the papers to Manuel a couple days ago. The ship belongs to him."

"That's rough. How you going to keep the business afloat?"

"With the Lord's help, we'll find a way. Good day, Mr. Dabney." Richard didn't hang around for an additional comment. Dabney was fishing for something. There probably wasn't another man representing Arcney Sponges. He didn't know how he knew, but he firmly believed Marc Dabney owned the other business.

At the house, he found his uncle and a room filled with the men to whom he'd loaned money. "Come in, Richard, these men are here to see you, not me."

The men nodded and waited for Richard to sit down. The spokesman of the group, David Zachary, cleared his throat. "Richard, we heard about the loss of the *Sea Dove* and we've dug up what we could, but I'm afraid it still won't cover the debt."

Richard looked at the itemized list of names and numbers. Each man had put down their debt and how much they had paid.

"We feel bad that you extended yourself so far on our accounts and lost the ship," David continued. "We can't do much, but anything we can do to help rebuild your warehouse, stock it, whatever, we're ready, willing, and able."

Richard didn't know what to say. "Thank you. Don't feel

badly about the ship, not that I won't be taking all of you up on your offers, mind you."

The tension in the room broke and the men started laughing. Ellis tapped him on the back and whispered, "Well done, Son."

"I could use a favor, though." The room hushed. "What do all of you know of Marc Dabney's businesses and Arcney Transport?"

"You borrow from him, he'll own you for life," Ben Greely offered.

"Thankfully, I noticed it on the contract long before I signed," Richard added.

"You know, I ain't never done business with the man. Avoided him actually, but I did find it odd he went to Cuba a week after the fire and didn't bring anything back with him. I thought for sure he'd have filled the ship and charged folks triple the asking price for it. Guess I might be wrong about the man."

A week after the fire? About the time Manuel got the offer from Arce Transport. "Has anyone known any of his businesses' names?"

"Afraid not," David put in. "He's one you need to watch yourself with. Something about a man who owns a business that no one sees. He's got an office and all, but nothing else."

"Interesting." Ellis rubbed his beard. "Why are you asking, Son?"

"I ran into him when I was leaving the bank today, saying he had a friend with some sponging skiffs for sale. His friend never showed, and his friend's business is Arcney Sponges."

"Arcney, that's the name I heard once," Ben offered.

"Arcney Transport was the name in real fine print on the contract Marc offered me."

"If we hear anything, we'll let you know." David rose to leave and extended his hand to Richard. "Pleasure doing business with you, Richard. If you need anything, don't hesitate to call on me."

"Thank you."

Each man gave his salutation, and when the dust settled behind them, Ellis walked back into the room and asked, "What was all of that about Marc Dabney?"

"I have a feeling he's behind the offer in Cuba, and I don't trust him about the skiffs. Here's the real interesting thing, Uncle Ellis. He knew I'd been to visit Nathaniel Farris. How could he? Nathaniel lives out from the center of town, and yet Dabney knew it right after I visited him. Granted, island gossip spreads faster than rain but. . ."

"But he may have had someone watching you," Ellis finished.

"Yeah, how'd you know?"

eighteen

"I've had similar thoughts in the past." Ellis sat down on the sofa. "Never any proof. I also wouldn't be surprised if some of the problems I've encountered over the years could be traced back to him. For the most part, nothing was substantial enough to warrant an investigation, mostly just annoying incidents."

"Do you suppose he stole the skiffs?"

"Possibly. But it might be more like him to mention to someone in need of cash the suggestion to steal the skiffs."

"Ah, so he never does his own dirty work?"

"Precisely."

"How can we catch him?"

"Other than catching him with the stolen skiffs, I doubt we can."

"He was real curious about why I was in the bank. Even Farley was concerned that I'd pull out the thirty-five thousand from my trust fund to secure the *Sea Dove*."

"I imagine he used it to loan the money to others." Ellis sat back.

"Right." Richard rolled his shoulders and stretched his neck from side to side. "I'm expecting Emile Fernandez this evening. He needs to speak with me about my ability to care for his daughter."

Ellis stifled a chuckle. "Is that why you were in the bank?"

"Yeah, I had them prepare a statement for me of my accounts there. I figure the monies there are more than enough. I shouldn't need to go into my other funds."

A knock on the door got Ellis on his feet. "Aptly spoken, Son. I believe you have a visitor."

Richard anxiously waited for his future father-in-law to enter.

"Thank you," Ellis responded to the unseen guest. "Relax," he called back. "It's a delivery from Nathaniel."

Cook, Bea, and his cousin Grace stepped from various rooms to see. "Well, ain't ya goin' to open it, Boy, and show us?" Cook asked.

Richard took the small box from his uncle and grinned. "I believe the receiver of the gift is the one to show you the ring."

"Oh, phooey, you're no fun," Grace pouted.

"All right, come here." Richard opened the box and carefully removed the rings. Nathaniel had outdone himself. The rings were beautiful. He'd even carved a curl in the wedding band to match the gentle twist to the engagement ring.

"Oh my, Richard, they are beautiful."

"Thanks, Nanna."

The women chattered about the rings until the door rattled again in its hinges. Richard braced himself. If Emile knocked that hard, then maybe he wasn't too happy about Isabella and him getting together.

"Buenas noches, Señor and Señorita Fernandez, *como están?"* Ellis greeted.

"Bien, Señor Southard," Emile answered. Isabella stood looking down at her feet. Richard fought every urge in his body to sweep her into his arms and hold her tight to reassure her everything would be all right.

"Come, sit in the front room, Señor Fernandez," Richard encouraged.

"Gracías, Richard."

He called me Richard. . .that's a start.

Isabella followed her father into the sitting room. Richard reached for her hand and squeezed it. It was the best he could offer. She turned to him, and he whispered, "I love you, my Bella."

"I love you too," she replied in a hoarse whisper.

"Richard, I've come to see if you can provide for my daughter," Emile announced.

Richard pulled out the envelope from his shirt pocket. "I went to the bank this morning and had them prepare this statement of my assets in their bank." He handed Emile the paper. "Forgive me for asking, but do you read English?"

"Not very well; that is why I've brought Isabella. This would normally be done without her present so as not to embarrass the child."

Richard nodded. *She is not a child.* Nanna stepped up beside him and handed him the ring box, which he promptly put in his trousers pocket. "The numbers will be the same, but to understand the terms, Isabella is very capable. She is also well aware of these statements."

Emile opened the envelope and looked over the figures. His eyes widened. Richard was certain the poor man had never earned in his entire life the balance of just one of his funds and never dreamed of their combined balance. Emile cleared his throat. "Am I understanding this is how much you have in the bank?"

"Yes, Sir, in this bank."

He handed the sheet of paper to his daughter. She looked over the numbers. "Sí, Papá, these are true figures."

In Spanish, Emile asked his daughter why she did not tell him, and she replied it wasn't her position to speak of another man's private financial matters. Reluctantly, Emile agreed. "I see you can care for my daughter financially more than I could ever give her, and you've shared your heart last night about your feelings for her. As she has shared with me also. I cannot turn down your request to marry my daughter, but I am not happy with how this came about."

Richard cleared his throat. "I ask your forgiveness in the forward manner in which I approached your daughter."

ex

Isabella's heart was breaking to see Richard so contrite and taking on her sin as his own. She wanted to protest. But her father would never understand that she was the one who had been forward.

"I am responsible for this dishonor I have caused your family. I know of no way to correct that wrong. I do love your daughter and would never compromise her, but my customs and yours differ so on this point."

Emile raised his gaze to face Richard one-on-one. "I have always respected you as a man of honor. To have spoken with Isabella on more than one occasion about private matters of the heart without a chaperone has taken some respect away. But to face me like a man, admit your wrong, and ask my forgiveness has shown me respect. I accept your apology, and I wonder when you would like to marry my daughter?"

Isabella stood breathless.

"I trust your judgment on that decision, Señor Fernandez. But may I ask that I be able to share a custom of mine with your daughter before we decide on the date?"

Emile tilted his head. Isabella wondered what custom Richard was speaking of.

"Sí, I will have to learn to be gracious with your American customs since you are to be my son."

"Gracías." Richard turned to Isabella and took her hand. He bent down on one knee and faced her. He rubbed the top of her hand ever so gently with the ball of his thumb. Her heart pounded with anticipation. "My Bella, would you do me the honor of becoming my wife? I love you so much, I can't imagine life without you by my side."

"Oh, Richard, I love you too. Yes," she answered and wanted to jump in his arms.

He reached into his pocket. "Then please accept this ring as a symbol of my commitment to you and a sign to the rest of the world that you belong to me."

Her hands trembled as he placed the ring on her finger and kissed the top of her hand. She opened her arms to him and he embraced her, kissing the small of her neck, sending shivers down her spine. Maybe it was best there was a room full of people to keep their passion in check.

"I love you, Bella, my sweet Bella."

Emile cleared his throat. Ellis Southard coughed. Richard reluctantly released her.

"I think a short engagement period would be in order," Emile offered.

Isabella flushed and saw the same crimson stain on Richard's face.

"Where will you live, Richard? You mentioned a farm in New York?"

"For now, I think Isabella and I should remain in Key West. When she is ready and we have the Lord's peace about it, we'll probably return to New York."

As much as Isabella shuddered at the thought of the cold, harsh winters in New York, she remembered the warmth of Richard's embrace and kiss. A slight smile crept up her cheek. She'd be staying warm in the winter.

"Señor Fernandez, is it proper for me to hold your daughter's hands and to kiss her?"

"Sí, you are engaged now. It is acceptable."

Richard grasped her hand and held her firmly. "Isabella, may I kiss you?"

She couldn't speak. Desire fluttered through her body. *Thank You, Lord, that Papá has agreed to a short engagement.* She nodded her head. Richard's sweet lips captured her own as she wrapped her arms around him, pulling him closer. He held the distance between them. He was right; there was a room full of people, and a time and a place would come when they could embrace more intimately.

❧

Richard needed every ounce of his willpower to pull away from Isabella and to refrain from pulling her into his chest, where she so clearly wanted to be.

Richard held her hand. "When. . ." He cleared his throat. "When would you like to set the date, Señor?"

Ellis and Bea were holding each other's hands on the sofa. Richard noticed the approval in their eyes.

"Three months. I should think that will be enough time for the women to get the dress made and for you to find a home for your bride."

"Three months it is." Admittedly, he had hoped for tomorrow. But three months would give him time to put things in order. One thing was certain: He'd have to find his future father-in-law a job in order to keep them in Key West. "Señor Fernandez, are you moving with your company to Tampa?"

"I have little choice." Emile sat back in his chair.

Richard encouraged Isabella to sit down in hers. "Then perhaps a wedding in one month would be more in order."

"One month?" Emile squeaked.

Richard's eyes widened. He hadn't meant to speak, but he'd spoken his thoughts out loud. His face flamed red with embarrassment. "Ah, yes, this way, Isabella wouldn't have to leave with you and your wife. But are you willing to stay in the area if we can find work for you?"

"Certainly, if it's work I can do and be proud of."

"What if we do this? We'll plan on the wedding in three months. But if you haven't found a new job in a week, we could move the wedding date up to just before you leave," Richard suggested.

Emile rubbed his chin. "I don't know; seems very quick. But you might have a point. To move Isabella up to Tampa only to have her move back in a couple months doesn't seem logical."

A few other matters surrounding wedding plans were discussed by everyone. Even Cook came in the room to add to the discussion. Richard pulled Isabella to a corner of the room. "Are you happy with this?"

"Yes. I'd like more time, but we don't have it. Even if I were to move to Tampa, we would not see each other very often."

"Oh, don't be too sure of that. I would move to Tampa and wait. I don't want you out of my sight." He watched her smile brighten. "Do you know how much I love you?"

"I'm learning." She winked.

"May you never stop." Richard pushed back the dark strands of her hair from her face. "Do you like the ring? Does it fit?"

"It is beautiful. When did you have time?"

"I saw Nathaniel Farris this morning and ordered it. He had the setting made, so it was just a matter of putting in the stones that I selected."

"It is wonderful. I will cherish it always. I have nothing to give you."

"You silly woman, you've given me everything by agreeing to marry me."

"Richard, the day I first spoke with you, the day after the fire, what were you thinking about? You seemed so distant, almost lost."

"I was trying to decide what to do with my life. I'm not cut out to be a sponge fisherman. I don't mind the work, but the smell. . ."

Isabella giggled.

"I really do want to return to New York and start building up the farmstead. Industry is changing. So many opportunities are up there, but most important is the soil. I'm happy with my hands buried deep in the dirt. I suppose this was the problem. I knew where my heart lay, and yet I had responsibilities to fulfill here. And I truly do love the island. It's a great place to grow up. But I'm more like my dad than my uncle in that respect. I love the land."

"Oh, Richard, I will go happily. I only need to be with you. I don't even need to work."

Richard chuckled. "As my wife, you do not need to work. Tell me, would your father think it rude of me to invite him to come work on the farmstead with us?"

"You'd want your in-laws about?" Isabella raised an eyebrow.

"I was thinking they would have their own wing of the house to live in. Isabella, this house is not even the size of the wing I would let your parents live in."

"Oh my. How did your family come to have all this money?"

"My mother was wealthy before she married my father. Her estate was put in my name when she was dying. My father inherited the farmstead and any other monies his parents had when they died. My uncle Ellis had to make his own way in the world. Once I was old enough to understand the details of my inheritance and came of age, I put a trust together of half of my father's inheritance and gave it to my uncle to be divided up for himself and his children. Uncle Ellis had not only taken care of everything, he'd continued to have the farmstead make a profit."

"Your uncle is a wise businessman, and you are very kind-hearted."

"I try to be fair. Uncle Ellis and Aunt Bea have taught me a lot about the responsibilities wealth brings to a family. Aunt Bea comes from a wealthy family herself."

"You'd never know your family was this wealthy. You don't act rich."

Richard chuckled. "That is probably the best compliment you could ever give me. Do you understand why I couldn't just rescue the boat?"

"Yes, it would have caused a terrible loss in your interest rates."

"More than that, Bella, the bank here wouldn't have had that money to lend others."

"Oh, my." She placed her hand lovingly on his shoulder. "I see what you mean. I hadn't thought of that before."

"Sometimes it is better for us to go without for awhile in order for the community as a whole to stay afloat. I don't think I can move our money immediately out of Key West. And if your parents decide to stay on the island, we will need to have some spending cash when we travel down here during the winter."

"What, and miss the snow?" she teased.

"You mentioned a verse of Scripture that first day. I've seen it played out in several ways over the past few weeks. First in Cook's life. As she lay on death's doorstep, everyone whom she had touched came to lend a hand, say a prayer, extend their love back to her. Tonight before your father came, the men on the island came over and gave what they could, hoping it would help us buy back the *Sea Dove*. It can't, but it will give us the much-needed money to rebuild the warehouse. They gave from their heart, not from duty."

Isabella added, "And just as you cast your bread upon the waters, it has returned to you."

"Yes and even more. How was I to know I would marry the lily of the ruins," he murmured into her ear. "You captured my heart that day. You stole it with just your presence. Now, it's returned to me fuller, richer, and wanting so much more. I love you, Isabella, my Bella."

"And I love you. Do you know your name means Dominant Ruler? How fittingly you were named, and how noble and honorable you have lived."

"Oh, Bella, my sweet, sweet Bella." He captured her lips once again and savored the sweet nectar. He could live off of those kisses for the rest of his days, and thankfully the Lord above had seen fit to give him such a sweet gift. *Thank You, Lord.*

epilogue

One year later

Richard held Isabella's hand as they stood beside Cook's grave. "I will miss her," Isabella whispered.

Tears burned his eyelids. "As will I. But over the past year she'd spoken with me a lot of her departure from this earth. She was looking forward to heaven; and I know it was her time to go."

"Yes, she was special."

A single tear slid down his cheek. "Yes, she was. I'm glad she was here long enough to see justice come to Marc Dabney."

"Who'd have thought he'd be so foolish as to try and sell you your own boats back?" Isabella snuggled into his chest.

"I think he'd gotten his mind so clouded by his sins, he no longer could see straight. It's a good thing we stopped him when we did or else he would have stolen Cook's family home as well. Thankfully, Cook was still alive and had the original paperwork on her property in Ellis's safe. I can't believe the forgeries the sheriff found in Dabney's files."

Richard placed his hand upon his wife's swollen belly. A child, their child, was growing within her. "Have I told you today how beautiful you are?"

"Only twice." She winked. They had said their good-byes to the island residents last night. Today they would sail for their new home in New York. Emile and Yolanda would soon be joining them.

Richard led her a step back from the grave and looked toward heaven, his throat thick with emotion. "Good-bye, Cook. We'll see you again in heaven, but not for a little while."

A Letter To Our Readers

Dear Reader:

In order that we might better contribute to your reading enjoyment, we would appreciate your taking a few minutes to respond to the following questions. We welcome your comments and read each form and letter we receive. When completed, please return to the following:

Rebecca Germany, Fiction Editor
Heartsong Presents
PO Box 719
Uhrichsville, Ohio 44683

1. Did you enjoy reading *One Man's Honor* by Lynn A. Coleman?

    ❏ Very much! I would like to see more books
       by this author!
    ❏ Moderately. I would have enjoyed it more if

    _____

    _____

2. Are you a member of **Heartsong Presents**? Yes ❏ No ❏
    If no, where did you purchase this book?_____

    _____

3. How would you rate, on a scale from 1 (poor) to 5 (superior),
    the cover design?_____

4. On a scale from 1 (poor) to 10 (superior), please rate the
    following elements.

    _____ Heroine   _____ Plot

    _____ Hero   _____ Inspirational theme

    _____ Setting   _____ Secondary characters

5. These characters were special because_____

_____

_____

6. How has this book inspired your life?_____

_____

_____

7. What settings would you like to see covered in future
   Heartsong Presents books?_____

_____

_____

8. What are some inspirational themes you would like to see
   treated in future books?_____

_____

_____

9. Would you be interested in reading other **Heartsong
   Presents** titles?   Yes ❑   No ❑

10. Please check your age range:
    ❑ Under 18   ❑ 18-24   ❑ 25-34
    ❑ 35-45   ❑ 46-55   ❑ Over 55

Name _____

Occupation _____

Address _____

City _____ State _____ Zip _____

Email _____

KANSAS

*S*urviving the harsh prairie elements—like surviving the storms of the heart—takes faith and determination, which four young women need to prove they possess. Can their hearts hold fast against the gales that buffet them? Will they find love waiting at the end of the storm?

Love on the Kansas prairie is hard and unpredictable. . .but also as inevitable as an early summer cyclone. Watch in wonder as God turns the storms of life into seasons of growth and joy.

paperback, 464 pages, 5 ³⁄₁₆" x 8"

♥ ♥ ♥ ♥ ♥ ♥ ♥ ♥ ♥ ♥ ♥ ♥ ♥ ♥ ♥ ♥ ♥ ♥

Please send me _____ copies of *Kansas*. I am enclosing $5.97 for each.
(Please add $2.00 to cover postage and handling per order. OH add 6% tax.)

Send check or money order, no cash or C.O.D.s please.

Name_____

Address _____

City, State, Zip _____

To place a credit card order, call 1-800-847-8270.
Send to: Heartsong Presents Reader Service, PO Box 721, Uhrichsville, OH 44683

♥ ♥ ♥ ♥ ♥ ♥ ♥ ♥ ♥ ♥ ♥ ♥ ♥ ♥ ♥ ♥ ♥ ♥

Hearts♥ng Presents
Love Stories Are Rated G!

That's for godly, gratifying, and of course, great! If you love a thrilling love story but don't appreciate the sordidness of some popular paperback romances, **Heartsong Presents** is for you. In fact, **Heartsong Presents** is the *only inspirational romance book club* featuring love stories where Christian faith is the primary ingredient in a marriage relationship.

Sign up today to receive your first set of four never-before-published Christian romances. Send no money now; you will receive a bill with the first shipment. You may cancel at any time without obligation, and if you aren't completely satisfied with any selection, you may return the books for an immediate refund!

Imagine. . .four new romances every four weeks—two historical, two contemporary—with men and women like you who long to meet the one God has chosen as the love of their lives. . .all for the low price of $9.97 postpaid.

To join, simply complete the coupon below and mail to the address provided. **Heartsong Presents** romances are rated G for another reason: They'll arrive *Godspeed!*